PARTNERS TO A DEGREE

BY HORST CHRISTIAN

Children To A Degree

Loyal To A Degree

Trust To A Degree

Partners To A Degree

PARTNERS TO A DEGREE

BASED ON A TRUE STORY

Horst Christian

This book is a work of fiction based on a true story.

PARTNERS TO A DEGREE

Copyright © 2014 Horst Christian

All rights reserved. No part of this publication may be reproduced, stored in a retrieval system or transmitted by any means including electronic, mechanical photocopying, recording, or otherwise, except brief extracts for the purpose of review, without the permission of the copyright owner.

www.horstchristian.com

First Printing 2014

ISBN-13: 978-1500406387

ISBN-10: 1500406384

For Harold. In memory of a true friend.

ACKNOWLEDGEMENTS

First of all, I would like to thank my readers for all their pertinent questions and who waited patiently for this book to be completed.

Christina Haas of ZenithBusinessSolutions again provided her invaluable guidance. She is always available when I need her help, including weekends and many off hours. As always, she did all the formatting for the different editions as well as the cover art. Her expertise is amazing and priceless. Thank you, Chris, especially for your constant and tireless encouragement. Every author should be so lucky to have an assistant like you.

Thank you, Nicole Etolen, for your editing skills and for keeping me on track with the story.

And last, but not least, I want to thank Jennifer, my helpful and supportive wife who again encouraged me to write in my comfortable office while she tended to the constant demand of our small ranch. Thank you, Jenny.

PREFACE

This book is based on a true story; however, the names of the characters have been changed. All of the characters are based on real people, each of the locations existed, and the events throughout the story actually took place

FOREWORD

The paths we travel in life and the people we become are influenced by our environment and our own personal experiences. A simple twist of fate is all it takes to alter our lives completely and send us down a new path. As young boys Karl, and his best friend Harold, led similar lives - until the circumstances of war changed everything. Two lives that once paralleled each other would eventually become as different as night and day.

Horst Christian, June 2014

One

Berlin, Germany. Second week in May 1945

Karl raced out of the Pompolit's (Soviet Political Kommissar) office. Not looking right or left, he jumped down the staircase taking three steps at a time. His friend Harold, who waited for him outside the door, didn't know what his haste was about and hurried behind him.

"Pappa," shouted Karl when he reached the rain-swept courtyard. "Father, how are you?"

The middle-aged man in the grey uniform of a German infantry soldier could hardly believe his eyes or ears. Three days ago he was among hundreds of other German soldiers in a POW camp in Berlin destined for labor camps in Siberia.

One day ago he had been separated from his unit and taken to an office building where he was kept in a clean, solitary confinement area and fed a decent meal. Now he was looking at his fourteen-year-old son. The last time he had seen him, Karl had been in his HJ uniform. This was over nine months ago and a lot of things had changed.

Berlin had been conquered by the Soviets and a week ago, WWII had ended. The majority of the Western Allies were still standing down on the Elbe River, except for a few units the Soviets allowed to proceed to Berlin. The Russians were already engaged in systematically shipping German POWs to labor camps in the Ural to build their railroad lines through the mountains.

"Pappa," cried Karl again as he threw his arms around his

father. Neither one of them could fully comprehend that they were actually seeing each other.

The Mongolian guard who had escorted the POW stood aside as Karl dragged his father out of the pouring rain into the shelter of the hallway.

"Harold, run up to the Kommissar and tell him that I will see him in a few minutes. I will be up after I talk with my father." Harold's eyes were open wide in surprise when he recognized Karl's father.

As Karl walked back up to Kommissar Godunov's office, he opened the door to a small room which served as a mess for the Mongolian unit occupying the old office building. He pulled up a chair and helped his father to get out of the heavy and wet infantry overcoat. It had been raining for the last few hours but the uniform under the coat was dry, indicating that his father must have been sheltered someplace out of the nasty weather.

"What kind of a building is this and what are you doing here?" Herr Veth was trying to clean his eyeglasses; still confused, he could not believe that he was actually with his son.

"I will answer you right away. But first tell me how and when you got here." Karl looked around the room to see if there was any food he could offer his father. "Are you hungry?" he asked. The door opened and a giant-looking Tatar entered the room. He placed a bowl of steaming soup on the table and then reached in his pocket to produce a spoon and a portion of black bread. He patted Karl on the shoulder and left the room only to return within a minute with a large teapot, several cups and a bowl of hard rock candy. He poured himself a cup of the hot liquid, stuck a piece of the rock sugar in his mouth and sat down on a bench to sip the tea through the sugar between his teeth.

Karl saw the questioning look on his father's face. "No, he does not understand German and you have nothing to fear from him. His name is Alex and he is more of a friend than a guard." He pushed the bowl of cabbage and onion soup toward his father, who had yet to answer any of his questions.

"Alright, I see that you are just as stunned as I am. All I can tell you at this moment is that we don't have much time for long explanations." Karl helped himself to some of the moist dark bread.

"We are being detained by a Russian Political Kommissar

named Godunov. The Mongols you see in this building are his personal bodyguards. They are a very small, independent political unit and not under the command of Colonel General Berzarin, the Russian city commander of Berlin." He paused for a moment to see if his father comprehended what he was saying.

"During the last days I had some assignments from the Kommissar which I finished to his satisfaction. At least I thought so until a few minutes ago when he asked me to complete a personal task for him. When I refused and bid him goodbye he seemed to be content, but then he announced that he knew your whereabouts and this was when I saw you standing in the courtyard."

Karl realized that his father was trying to follow his short report.

"What kind of a task did you refuse?" asked Herr Veth.

"I can't tell you right now. But I have a feeling that our freedom might depend on it. As I said before, we have very little time. Please tell me when and how you arrived at this building."

Karl could not tell his father what the Pompolit had asked of him. It would have taken hours to explain the entire situation. The events unfolded too fast and he desperately needed some time to think. But most of all, he wanted to know how long his father had been detained under the command of Godunov.

"I was questioned by a Russian officer two days ago just when our camp was readied for a train transport. Curiously enough, he never asked about my Volksturm unit or my service record. All he wanted was information about my family and I remember now that he asked me if I had a son in the HJ." Herr Veth tried to recall the interrogation.

"When did you get here?" Karl repeated his original question.

"I was separated from my unit yesterday afternoon. Two Mongols came with a truck and drove me to this building. They gave me a nice clean room with a folding bed." Herr Veth had finished his soup and tried some of the tea.

"And then?" pressed Karl.

"They left me alone until about two hours ago. Then, a Mongol handed me my coat and made me stand in the hallway and then later a different Tatar came and I had to stand in the rain in the courtyard."

While the timing made sense to Karl, he was unsure about the exact motive behind the Kommissar's actions. Was Godunov about to release his father as a reward for his previous actions or was he using him as a threat to force him into obedience? There was only one way to find out. He had to talk with him.

"I have to go to see Godunov. I will be back shortly." Karl got up to leave the room.

"Hold on, Karl, I have a thousand questions. Have you heard from Mother and what will happen to us?" Herr Veth looked pleadingly at his son.

"I heard from Mother. She took little Willy and Monika and is someplace safe in Westphalia. When I come back I might know more about our future but right now, I really do not know, Pappa. You might remember my friend Harold. He is also here. If I find him I will send him to you to bring you up to date." Karl hated to leave his father so shortly after their reunion but he had no choice. He knew that the Kommissar was waiting for him.

Karl motioned to the huge Tatar to keep his seat. Harold came in just as Karl was about to leave the room.

"Godunov wants to see you," Harold announced.

Karl nodded. "Please answer my father's questions. I trust that my conversation with the Kommissar will be rather short."

Karl tried to clear his mind as he was going up the stairs to face the Pompolit. Until about two hours ago he had been on good terms with the political Kommissar. But now it seemed as if the situation had changed.

Kete, the Tatar standing guard in front of the Pompolit's office, nodded at Karl and opened the door to let him enter.

The Kommissar, a broad-shouldered and grey-haired officer in his late forties, looked up when Karl entered and pointed to a chair in front of his desk.

"Sit down, Karl. I know that you are excited and maybe upset with me." He spoke in a nearly perfect German. "However, if you listen to me you will understand that this isn't what it seems to be."

To say that Karl was excited and upset was a vast understatement. He had so many questions that he didn't know where to start.

But, he was in no way fooled by the polite words of the Pompolit. He decided to bide his time and wait for the Kommissar to begin.

To Karl's astonishment, the Pompolit dragged his chair in front of the desk to sit almost next to Karl. By now Karl was used to the various techniques of the Russian intelligence officer, but this subliminal gesture of companionship was a new one to him. Warning bells were going off in his mind and he decided to listen very carefully.

"When you stormed out of my office to greet your father, you seemed to be under the impression that I tried to force your hand. However, this was not my intention."

In spite of his earlier decision, Karl was unable to keep his mouth shut.

"With all due respect, Herr Godunov, you wanted me to eliminate a Russian officer and when I refused, you told me that you knew where my father was. What was I supposed to think?"

The Kommissar smiled at Karl. "Exactly. I wanted you to think that I was using your father to change your mind. And, I still intend to do that, but in a more benign way than you expect."

Karl studied the Kommissar without answering. He'd known him since the surrender of Berlin, which was about two weeks ago, and he knew that the Russian officer never wasted any time getting to the point. He was waiting to hear him out.

"Let me explain." The Kommissar moved his chair a little to the side which allowed him to reach for a piece of paper covered with handwritten notes. "You and Harold did some important work for me and you also told me that you were searching for your parents. Because of your excellent work I decided to help you boys and you know that I found Harold's mother." He looked at his notes.

"As of two days ago I was informed of your father's whereabouts. He was a member of a POW transport which left today for the Ural Mountains. I used my authority on your father's behalf and yesterday I was able to obtain his release into my custody. It was my intent, and still is, to grant him his freedom. I wanted to reward you for finding my daughter." Godunov was done with his notes. He placed them back on his desk.

"As of last night I knew the identity of the bastard who nearly killed her. I also realized that I was unable to avenge her and I asked for your help. When you refused I told you that I knew where your father was." The officer locked eyes with Karl. "When you ran out of the office you yelled at me '*you win*'. It was *you* who assumed that I was using your father as a tool to achieve my objective. I never said a word to lead you to that conclusion."

Karl didn't blink when he returned the officer's stare.

"That was, in essence, what happened. However, you asked me to shoot and kill a Russian officer. When I answered that I don't kill and that I was not about to change my values you wished me '*Good Luck*' and only then you produced my father."

His face gave nothing away as he decided to give the impression of being helpless, and he slowly looked around the office. "Herr Godunov, you are an experienced interrogation officer. Please tell me what did you expect me to think?"

"Of course I wanted you to think that I was using your father and your loyalty to him to achieve my objective. I had to confuse you sufficiently enough to make you reconsider."

The Pompolit was obviously satisfied with himself and looked keenly at Karl who got up from his chair and started to pace the room. It seemed to him that Godunov had finished his explanation and waited for him to ask questions. Karl always had questions. Plenty of them. But, the present subject required only a few. Karl always thought of his questions like pawns in a chess game and in this particular game his father's security was the primary object. Everything else was secondary.

"First of all, I would like to thank you for finding my father, Herr Godunov. And, if I understand you correctly, Herr Godunov, you are willing to release my father even if I don't agree to help you to eliminate your personal enemy."

He purposely used the word 'eliminate' instead of 'kill'. For him these were two distinctly different actions.

"Exactly, Karl. Your father is free to go." The Kommissar answered slowly and then added: "However, the Zampolit Sodbileg Kozlov is not my personal enemy. I never had a quarrel with him until last week when he raped my daughter and nearly killed her. I think that he acted in his normal drunken stupor and I doubt very much that he even knew that she is a Russian medical officer. I am sure that he does not know that she is my daughter."

Now it was Godunov who could not sit still anymore and paced the room.

"But, yes, I want him to pay for what he did, not only to my Anna but also to countless other helpless women. I want him eliminated and I told you that due to his powerful connections in Moscow my hands are tied. Neither my unit, nor I personally, are able to do this."

Karl had the distinct feeling that he was being cornered into a compromise.

"I understand your situation, Herr Godunov." Karl stopped at the window. The rain had stopped beating against the panes and it was nearly dark outside.

"I would like to take my father to some friends and I'll be back tomorrow to assist you." Karl was not really sure where to take his father or for that matter how to help the Kommissar. It had served him before not to over-think a problem and at the moment, he just wanted to make sure his father was safe and not in danger of being transported to Russia.

The Kommissar sat down again. "You are free to take your father wherever you wish, but be aware that the Belorussian troops are still busy scouring the houses. They are searching for German deserters and able men to ship to the Ural. Your father has a better chance of freedom staying right here, under my protection."

Karl knew that Godunov was right. None of the regular Russian troops or officers would dare to bother the high ranking Pompolit. He also knew that Godunov wanted to know details about Karl's offer of assistance. He figured it might be best to comply with the Kommissar's suggestion and leave his father where he was for another day.

"Please allow me to talk with my father for a minute. I'll be back up in a moment." He was already at the door when he turned around. "Is it possible that my father can share Harold's and my room?"

"Yes, of course. I will instruct Kete accordingly." The Kommissar started to talk to Kete as Karl headed down to the mess room.

He found his father far more relaxed than when he had left him.

"I answered your father's questions as well as I could," Harold looked up at Karl. "How was your meeting with Godunov?"

Karl ignored the question from his friend for a moment. He walked up to his father and hugged him over and over again.

"I am so glad to see you alive, Pappa. Your time as a prisoner is pretty much over. The Kommissar assured me of your freedom.

It will not take long and we will be on our way to see Mutti." He smiled at his father. "Tonight you will sleep in our room and we can talk as long as you wish. In the meantime, I need Harold to go with me to see the Pompolit once more."

Kete entered the room carrying some civilian clothing for Herr Veth and then motioned him to follow. He kind of grunted at Alex to give him a hand with a folding cot and all three of them proceeded up to the boys' sleeping quarters.

Karl stopped short of Godunov's office. He needed to inform his friend of the Pompolit's latest request. Harold thought he had not heard correctly. "Godunov wants you to shoot a Russian officer and you agreed?"

"No, I only agreed to assist him with his needs. No specifics have been discussed. I need you to help me think how I will be able to do this."

Harold listened in bewilderment. A day or two ago he had accepted a generous adoption offer from Godunov. The offer had been fully in the interest of the Kommissar and included a formal Soviet education. He was already receiving Russian language tutoring and was wearing a Russian uniform. Identification papers had been issued which identified him as a protégé of Pompolit Godunov.

One of the reasons that Harold accepted the offer was the fact that his mother had not survived a brutal night of being raped by drunken Soviet soldiers. He thought that by joining up with Godunov he might have a chance of avenging her death. His father was missing and for all he knew he might be dead too. Besides, he saw no future for himself in Germany.

The Pompolit, on the other hand, knew exactly what he was doing by recruiting a young German ally.

Two

Godunov looked astonished at the two boys when they entered his office.

"I did not expect to see you, Harold, but it seems that Karl wants you involved. So it is fine with me."

He was in his chair behind his desk and waived at the boys to take a seat.

"Before we start I have some good news and some not so good news for you, Harold." He looked intently at his protégé. Harold braced himself for the bad part of the news.

"I found more information about your father. We knew that he was being held captive in Spandau but now we also know that he is well and in good shape. The not so good news is that he has been classified as a political prisoner. As a German civilian official he will be tried for war crimes. At this time I don't know where the war crime tribunal will be held but I am told that it will not be in Berlin."

He locked eyes with Harold and saw the questioning look. "No, Harold, I am sorry. I am unable to get him out of Spandau. There is an agreement between the four super powers that all the German political prisoners will be under a joint guard. This means that there are French, British, US and Soviet guards on duty. I have no power to override them or to make a deal with them."

The Kommissar pushed himself back a bit from his desk, pulled out a side drawer and rested his legs on top of it.

"Herr Godunov, how severe and how long do you expect the prison terms to be?" Karl ventured a question on behalf of his friend.

"I am told that none of the political prisoners will be delegated to labor camps. Supposedly, they will remain in German prisons. As to the terms, I have no idea. But my guess is that the minimum term will be in excess of five years for the most benign cases and the worst will be death by hanging."

"But, my father is not a criminal. He was only in charge of food and material distribution. If anything, he should get a medal for keeping order in the supply chain." Harold's eyes were moist as he voiced his protest.

Godunov studied the boy for a moment and then slowly proceeded to answer.

"Harold, if the Germans would have won the war your father might have received a medal, however, since the Germans are the losers he will probably be found guilty of a war crime."

Karl felt sorry for his friend and tried to think of something positive to say.

"Look at the bright side of it, Harold. If it would not have been for the Kommissar you would still not know the whereabouts of your father or that he is even alive. Now, you not only know that he is well but you also know that he will not be sent to a labor camp in Russia."

Harold wiped his eyes. "Thank you Herr Godunov for bringing me the news." His voice was steady and he silently thanked his friend for pointing out the good part of the message.

"But, may I ask how you found out about him?" he addressed the Kommissar.

"That was easy, Harold. You told me that your father had been evacuated from Berlin with some other civilian government officials. After I found your mother, I persisted in getting information about the male detainees." He reached for a plain piece of paper and a pen. "Here, take this and when you are alone, write a cheerful note to your father telling him that you are uninjured and well. Do not tell him about your mother. I cannot promise you anything except that I will endeavor to get this message to him."

Harold thanked him again and kept quiet as the Kommissar turned his attention to Karl.

"You told me about your values and that you do not kill. You were very adamant about it. I believe you. However, you know that I want the Zampolit Kozlov dead and a few minutes ago you offered to assist me. Please tell me what you intend to do."

Karl had several ideas and answers to this question but first, he wanted to know more about Kozlov.

"You told me that Sodbileg Kozlov is a well-connected Zampolit and that this is the reason you are unable to eliminate him yourself. I never heard of a Zampolit. Could you please explain?"

"Of course, Karl. A Zampolit is like me, a political officer. His title infers that he is a deputy commander. He is on the career path of the Communist party and not subject to the military command."

"Then what is the difference between a Zampolit and a Pompolit?" Karl wanted to know.

"Not much of a difference; we are both party men, except that a Zampolit acts as a deputy and is required to wear a military uniform while a Pompolit is tasked with the overall party protocol and is allowed to wear civilian clothing in a peacetime environment."

"You also indicated to me that this Kozlov is an incompetent drunk and his only claim to fame are his untouchable connections to Moscow," Karl continued.

"It is not so much that he is a drunk than what he does when he is in a stupor. He is directly responsible for countless murders and rapes besides making up trumped up charges to have his opponents sent to political prisoner labor camps in Siberia. Even his associates will breathe easier when he ceases to exist."

While Karl was evaluating what he had heard, Harold suddenly showed interest in the conversation. He could not help but join in. "I think that I understand. You don't want Karl to shoot the man. You just want him dead."

Godunov did not answer him directly but nodded his head in agreement.

"I also assume from your previous remarks that you need complete and absolute deniability since the rape of your daughter could possibly be linked to the sudden demise of Kozlov."

"This is correct, Harold. Any suggestions?"

"Nothing. Not a single thing. You just confirmed that you want complete deniability. Therefore, I suggest nothing. But, I recall that you told us that the City Commander of Berlin, Colonel General Berzarin, invited you to a belated victory celebration in a few days. Will the Zampolit participate?"

"I know the party is scheduled for the day after tomorrow and it will only be for a select group of officers. Due to Kolovos position I think that it is a given that he will be invited."

"Will you be allowed to bring your guards with you?"

"Not only allowed, it will be expected of me. But none of them will participate in the festivities. Their presence will be strictly for security," Godunov confirmed.

"Perfect," beamed Harold, "now please tell me where this Zampolit's headquarters is located."

"He seemed to have stayed only one night in Potsdam where he raped my daughter. He is presently occupying a small estate in a suburb of Berlin called Gatov." Godunov pulled a small map from a shelf and opened it on the desk.

"We visited Gatov once on a work detail," Karl remembered.

"Yeah," agreed Harold. "We don't need a map. Gatov is very small and I can only think of one particular place that could possibly qualify as an estate."

"Kind of strange that a high ranking victorious officer is holed up in this out of the way area," Karl remarked.

"No, not really," disagreed the Kommissar. "A few weeks ago the Zampolit stayed at a decrepit area by Warsaw. It was similar last year in Hungary. He likes small out of the way places to entertain his friends with female prisoners. He could not do this in the middle of a city where his orgies might be subjected to interruptions."

Harold studied the map. It was an old outdated edition, showing the greater area of Berlin. Gatov was only a name on it, close to the town of Spandau without any details of the surroundings.

"This does not tell me much," he said to the Kommissar and pushed the map away.

"Thinking back I remember enough of the village. Besides, I don't need to see the place anyway." Harold smiled at his friend. "I need a few minutes to talk with you before you visit with your father."

Karl was glad that the meeting was coming to an end before

he had to give the Kommissar any assurances.

"May we be excused until tomorrow? He looked at Godunov, who was equally anxious to spend the remainder of the evening with his daughter. He was already thinking how he could feasibly assure her safety. Maybe he could use his influence to separate her from her unit. Now that the war was over, he could possibly dismiss her from active duty and send her back for advanced studies to the Moscow Institute of Medicine.

Then again, he knew his daughter. If she was bent on revenge it would be very difficult for him to convince her to go back to Russia. His only practical solution was to eliminate Kozlov before his daughter decided to take matters into her own hands. He had hoped that Karl would jump at the opportunity to take a shot at a Russian officer. The thought that the HJ-trained sniper might have moral values never occurred to him. Fortunately it seemed that Harold, who was bent on avenging his mother anyhow, did not share Karl's scruples.

"I will see you tomorrow morning. I still have the American Jeep at my disposal and I will instruct Poti to stand by if you want to travel to Gatov."

Although Harold was opening the door, Karl hesitated for a moment. "How is your daughter doing, Herr Godunov?" he wanted to know.

"She is resting comfortably. Thank you for asking, Karl."

The Pompolit liked the boys. He had no friends who would have bothered to inquire about the health of his daughter. All he had were some good associates. Good, but not close enough that he would trust them with his personal difficulties.

"Do you still have some of your Argentine miracle wound ointment? Anna might need it," he asked Karl.

The boy reached in his shirt pocket and handed the Kommissar a small vial with an oily substance. "You only need three or four drops and don't forget to dilute it with vegetable oil. Apply it directly to the wound."

"Thank you, Karl. Go and enjoy the visit with your father. I will see you tomorrow at 7:00 AM."

*****

"Do you want some time alone with your dad?" Harold asked as the boys walked through the hallway to their room.

"No, thank you, Harold. I don't need any privacy and I think that we should enjoy this evening together."

He stopped and faced his friend. "You wanted to ask me something or talk with me before we see my dad."

"Yeah, I will make it short. I'd like to take care of Godunov's problem."

"What do you mean by *take care of?*"

"Come on Karl, don't act so stupid. I might have used the wrong words, but I know that you would never kill anyone and also that you would never be an accomplice to an assassination."

"But you would?" Karl studied his friend, not quite sure what to make of Harold's offer. He had thought that they shared the same values. Obviously he was wrong.

"No, not directly anyway. But I can think of a way to keep Godunov and us completely out of it. And still, the Zampolit will get what he deserves."

"Alright, let's hear what you've got." Karl was curious.

"No, Karl, you don't need to know any of this. Just cover for me tomorrow because I will need the Jeep and Poti for a few hours. Please don't worry about me. Nothing will happen during that time."

"So, we are back to our old routine. One of us gets the job done while the other one is not allowed to ask questions," Karl summed it up.

"Exactly," confirmed Harold.

"Hmm, I don't know. Really, I don't know, Harold." Karl tried to envision what his friend had in mind.

"What exactly is causing you to hesitate?" Harold asked patiently. "I don't ask for anything and it always worked between us before."

"Yes, I know. But this time it's different than confiscating a motorcycle or obtaining medicine or food. This time we are talking about a human life."

"Alright then. I'll step back and you tell me your plan."

It seemed to Karl as if his friend was serious. "That's just it; I don't have a plan, yet. I am unable to think of anything except how to get my father away from the Soviet-controlled area to the Western Allies."

"Then that's it," announced Harold. "You concentrate on a

strategy to get your father to your mother and then, like always, you will also find a solution for the Kommissar's situation."

"So, we are clear then?" Karl wondered about his friend's apparent change of mind.

"Yes we are. Nonetheless, if Godunov's problem gets solved in the meantime then he is happy and you have no obligations."

Karl understood and knew when to back off. "I already know how to cover for you tomorrow," he said as he opened the door to their room.

*****

Herr Veth had discarded his old uniform and looked almost refreshed in the civilian clothes. The only odd things on him were the badly worn German army boots. Karl made a mental note to remedy this as soon as possible.

While Herr Veth had made a list of questions which he now consulted - after all he was a pedantic engineer - Karl had almost none. He was just joyful to see his father alive and well. As he listened to his father's recollection of the past year, his mind was occupied with the question of how to reunite his father with his mother. In order to achieve this he had to more or less smuggle his father through the Soviet-controlled zone and then through the western zone to Westphalia. He knew that the Soviet occupation zone was supposed to end on the Elbe River, about 160 Kilometers (100 miles) west of Berlin. But he knew nothing about the Western Allies other than the fact that they didn't ship their prisoners of war to Russia. Maybe they shipped them to America, but this did not sound as threatening as Siberia.

So he fielded his father's questions about the last few months and only now and then added one of his own. He gathered that his father's Volkssturm unit - Hitler's final call to arms, regardless of age - had not been engaged in the defense of Berlin. His regiment had been surrounded by the Belorussian armies near the Spreewald (a small river forest, outside of Berlin) and surrendered after they had run out of ammunition. This was about six weeks ago and luckily for his father the Soviets had still taken prisoners. Since then they had been kept in POW camps where they were fed one meal a day and were forced to sleep under the open sky. Nearly a week ago they had been transported to Berlin where his regiment was divided into future labor brigades waiting for their final deportation to Russia.

Herr Veth was still unable to fully comprehend his sudden freedom and repeated over and over his questions regarding his son's relationship with the political Kommissar. In spite of Harold's earlier explanations, there were many gaps which needed clarification.

"How did you obtain your position with the Pompolit?" he asked his son again. It must have been at least the fifth time.

Karl saw that his answers were insufficient for his father. At least at the present time. He decided on a question of his own: "You don't think of me and Harold as traitors, do you?"

His father shook his head. "No, not at all, but I still don't understand how the Kommissar feels he owes you my freedom."

"Well, Pappa, I don't know either. Our relationship is not normal, I know that much. It just evolved to the present state and this is the reason why I want to leave with you as soon as possible. Do you by any chance have any friends between here and Detmold in Westphalia where Mother is waiting for us?"

Herr Veth did not have to think before answering that question. He had no friends or relatives outside of Berlin. It was his wife who had relatives in Detmold.

"Is Harold coming with us?" he asked. Karl hesitated for a second and decided on a simple answer.

"No. Harold's father is in a political prison in Spandau. So he will be waiting for him here, in Berlin." He didn't tell his father about the rape and death of Harold's mother.

Their conversation ebbed on and off until after midnight. When Karl finally fell asleep he was at ease and happy. It had been a long, long time since his last peaceful sleep.

*****

Godunov had followed the instructions Karl gave him and mixed a few drops of the ointment with a few drops of vegetable oil. He handed the oily lotion to his daughter and asked her to carefully apply it to her cuts which refused to heal. He had observed the strange healing power of the ointment when Karl had tended to Alex's feet. The otherwise healthy and giant Tatar had suffered extensive wounds from marching hundreds of miles in badly fitting footwear. But now his feet were in excellent shape and the Kommissar had watched the Mongolian ritual in which Alex had thanked Karl. He knew that Karl had a friend for life in the simple but devoted Tatar.

Anna was aching when she tried to apply the liquid but as soon as the ointment touched her wounds it seemed that the pain was somehow numbed. As a physician herself she tried to understand what might cause the soothing sensations.

"Where did you get this medication?" she asked.

"I received it from my young German friend who obtained it from a submarine commander as a gift. We don't know anything about it except that it works wonders."

"If the lessening of the pain is not just temporary, then you might be correct and I would like to get the remainder analyzed." Anna closed her eyes as she started to enjoy a nearly painless sleep.

Three

It was shortly before seven in the morning when the boys met with Godunov in his office. Herr Veth was still sound asleep when Karl got up. He had told his father the previous evening that it would be late afternoon until he returned to plan their next move.

"The car is ready for you. I expect you back by noon because I want Harold to continue his language lessons."

The Pompolit addressed Karl who looked at Harold to confirm whether or not this was a sufficient amount of time.

"Who else will be with us besides your driver?" Harold wanted to know.

"Your choice. Either Alex or Kete. But I don't want them to be seen in Gatov. They might be too easily remembered in case something happens to the Zampolit."

"Nothing will happen in Gatov. We might not even go there," Karl objected, but the Kommissar was not convinced.

It turned out that the boys really had no choice. As soon as Alex realized that Karl was going for a ride he insisted on going along. Kete assigned a different Tatar to look after Herr Veth and stayed with Godunov.

"Where are we going?" Karl was glad that the Mongols decided to keep the top up on the Jeep. The rain from the day before had caused the dust on the streets to disappear and the sun did its best to warm up the city, but the morning was still cold.

"Never mind that '*we*' business," Harold said. "I will drop you and Alex off at the Becker's apartment and pick you up again in a few hours."

PARTNERS TO A DEGREE

Karl didn't object. Frau Becker, a former school teacher, had been very helpful during the last weeks. He wanted to see her anyway. It was only two days ago that Karl had found a group of homeless KLV (air evacuation camp) children who had been abandoned by their teachers and Frau Becker had assured him that she would look for their relatives. Herr Becker, a WWI invalid, opened the door when the Jeep drove up.

"My wife is with the children. She established a shelter for them in the church at the Hohenzollern Dam," he announced to the boys.

"Do you want me to take you there?" Harold asked Karl.

"No. Go and do what you need to do. Just in case we get questioned later, you stayed with me the whole time," Karl answered and went to look after Alex, who had finally mastered the indoor plumbing but was still fascinated by it.

The bathroom in the Becker's apartment had become his favorite place. About a week ago he had lost his underwear by flushing the commode where he had washed his shirts and he still looked for it every time he had a chance. But, it remained gone, never to resurface again.

Harold conferred with Herr Becker for a moment, who was very accommodating at first, but was then surprised by the questions. More than once he stole a look at Harold's Russian uniform. While his answers were slow and short, they seemed to satisfy Harold who thanked him and decided to take off without saying goodbye to Karl. The tentative answers from the veteran told him to get on the way before Karl could join the discussion and start asking follow up questions.

"I don't like Harold's enquiries. Do you have any idea what he is up too?" Herr Becker was uncomfortable. He wavered, unsure if he should bring up the questions Harold had asked.

Karl did not seem interested. "I don't want to know. Harold has his own agenda for this morning."

"I'll say, he does." The old man pulled up a chair. He needed to sit down. "Did anything happen yesterday that I should know?"

"Yes, Herr Godunov found my father, who is a POW. He tells me that he is willing to release him anytime I wish." Karl pulled up a chair for himself.

"Congratulations, Karl. This is great news. But you don't

trust the Kommissar?" Herr Becker beamed at Karl and ventured a guess.

"No, in this regard I trust him just fine. I just don't trust the Russian teams that are still roaming the streets."

The veteran nodded his head. "You are right to be careful. We just endured a detailed search of our apartment this morning; otherwise I would suggest that you bring him here."

Karl had hoped his friends would be able to hide his father; at least for a while until he could figure out how to get him out of Berlin. Based upon the old man's comment he had to rethink his options.

"Have you ever been to Magdeburg or Wittenberg?"

"Yes, I have. Years ago during a vacation trip to the Elbe River. Are you planning to take him to the Western Allies?" Herr Becker got up and searched his bookshelf for a map of Germany. "There are two direct routes and one of them is part of the Autobahn system. They will, without a doubt, be heavily controlled."

"Yeah," agreed Karl. "We will have to work our way through the countryside. Do you have any friends or relatives between here and the Elbe River?" He still hoped that Herr Becker could help him. One way or another.

The old man shook his head. "Not really, Karl. Sorry. You know that I would like to help you." He studied his map. "I wonder if these major highways are even passable. Chances are that the bombings and artillery shelling made a mess of them. However, come to think of it, I believe that my wife has a relative in the area of Magdeburg. I will ask her when she comes home."

Karl was not too sure that a contact in Magdeburg would be of any help to him. He was trying to think of other places where he could hide his father. He knew plenty of small hiding places in the subway system but they would only be good for a very short time.

He might as well leave his father right where he was right now. On the other hand, this was hardly a long term option. Herr Godunov had told him that he had received orders to leave Berlin within a few days.

"Let me see the map, please," Karl wanted to take a look at the secondary roads leading west. There were many and he tried to estimate how long he would have to walk with his father to reach the river. The figures he came up with looked pretty disappointing. He knew that a straight out march without interruptions was not possible. He could not even guesstimate if and when or where and for how long he would have to hide along the way.

"You know Karl, this is not really as bad as it looks." Herr Becker seemed to think differently and wanted to cheer up the boy. Karl looked up, waiting for the remainder of the good news.

"The distance is only between 150 and 180 Kilometers. (About 100 miles). Depending, of course, where you are able to cross the river. Even with hiding out along the way, you should reach the Elbe within 10 days, two weeks at the most."

Karl had to agree that less than 14 days was absolutely doable. Under normal conditions. But if the roads were swarming with Soviet troop then two weeks were not feasible. And where would he find food?

"May I take the map along? I mean for good because I would be unable to return it."

"Sure. Keep it. We are not going anywhere." Herr Becker got up and walked to the door. "Let's go and ask our neighbor. She might know of some contact outside the city."

Karl remembered the young mother and her little nine-year-old girl. It was a few days ago that Alex and Kete had saved them from getting raped by Mongolian soldiers.

The walk to their apartment was a bit tricky. Some Soviet bulldozers had cleared the center of the street and in doing so had pushed the debris from the destroyed buildings right up to the front doors. There were still some Mongolian women combing through the ruins and rubble for valuables, but the killing and raping had stopped. Not so much because of strict orders from Marshal Zhukov who wanted to end the slaughter and vandalism but more due to the fact that there were no more wounded German soldiers laying around.

"Good to see you well and relaxed," Karl greeted the neighbor woman politely before Herr Becker started to ask about relatives or other contacts outside Berlin.

"I have an aunt by Magdeburg. I never visited her, so I don't know if it is close to the river. I'd be happy to give you her address and a note of introduction." The woman was eager to help.

"See, there is one person. Let's go from house to house and

ask some of the other neighbors. We should be able to find you some assistance."

The invalid wanted to keep on going and Karl appreciated the effort but in spite of talking to a handful of other people, he didn't gain another contact.

It seemed that Harold was only gone for a short time but it was nearly noon when he returned with Poti.

"I am still not done," he grinned, unmistakably satisfied with his accomplishment of the morning. "I need civilian clothing and at least another hour. You can have the car and Poti."

Karl didn't question him. When Harold was in high gear, it was best not to interrupt him. He just signaled at Alex and Herr Becker to follow him and was ready to take off with the Jeep when Harold stopped him.

"Not so fast. Give me a moment to change into shorts and knee socks and then drop me off behind the Anhalter railroad station. Pick me up again in less than an hour."

Karl gave him quizzical look. "I don't want to know?"

"Right, no, you don't want to know." He finished changing his clothes and jumped in the back seat. "Go, go, go." His eyes glittered in some kind of anticipation.

Karl directed Poti to the badly damaged railroad station. A few days ago it had been a very busy place serving as one of the open air prison camps for former SS members. Since then most of the POW's camps had been consolidated and moved to the few still-functioning rail yards. Shipments of cattle cars full of prisoners left on a daily, nearly hourly basis. All of them bound for labor camps in the Soviet Union.

Many of the prisoners had refused to board the trains and just as many had simply been shot. Executed without mercy. Refusing the orders of prison guards was a death sentence in itself.

Because of this horror, the area around the former station building was practically deserted of German civilians as well as Russian soldiers, except for two old men towards the rear of the building. One of them limped with a wooden leg and the other had his left sleeve pinned to the shoulder, unmistakably WWI veterans.

When Harold spotted them he ducked down and tapped Karl on the arm. "Back to the front of the building. Go slow and I drop out".

Karl had Poti turn around and slow down in front of the station.

"Pick me up a block north of here. Thirty minutes. Be there. Please," Harold hissed at Karl and his eyes pleaded with him as he jumped out.

"Nice going", remarked Herr Becker as Poti picked up speed. "Where are we going now?"

"Home," Karl looked back but Harold had already disappeared in the rubble.

"I wanted you to meet Herr Reichert, another WWI veteran I know but now we don't have the time for it." He directed the driver back to the apartment. He wanted to be alone with the Tatars when he picked up Harold.

His friend's eyes had told him that things might get dicey.

Neither Poti nor Alex had given any indication that they cared about Harold or his actions. Their stoic faces hardly ever changed expression but Karl was sure that Alex would have followed him if he had jumped out of the jeep.

"I'll return with Harold. I am sure he will want his uniform back."

He didn't miss waving goodbye to Herr Becker but his mind was already ahead of the car. Harold wanted him back in 30 minutes and he had said *'please'*, enough of a hint to be prepared to search for him in case he didn't show up.

Karl tried to communicate the gravity of the situation to Alex and Poti. While the driver gave no indication that he understood, it seemed that Alex was also anxious to see Harold again.

One block north of the station? There was no regular housing block that would have matched the description. Nothing but plenty of ruins without a visible difference between former streets and collapsed buildings.

Karl was sure of his timing as the Jeep rolled a second time through the wreckage north of the station. No Harold, or for that matter, anyone else walking around. There were, however, plenty of American trucks crossing the station plaza and Karl's as well as the Tatars' eyes opened wide when they recognized that some of the soldiers were of a dark skin color. Poti almost ran into the side of a ruin when he saw that one of the drivers was definitely black.

Karl still considered it unbelievable and he felt sorry for the many young children in Berlin who were scared that the black American soldiers would eat them. They had seen their mothers being raped and some of them killed by the Mongolian soldiers, so getting eaten by black soldiers was a real possibility for them. After all, Hitler's propaganda machine had been very effective at proclaiming that it was better to throw themselves with explosives underneath a tank and die as a young hero than falling alive into the hands of the enemy.

Some of the American soldiers waved at them when they recognized the red Soviet star on the side and on the hood of the American built Jeep, and Karl understood why Poti nearly lost control of the vehicle. A deep black skinned face with smiling and sparkling white teeth was nothing he had ever seen before either.

By now, Poti understood that they were looking for Harold and drove a tighter circle close to the abandoned and twisted rail beds. Karl knew that Harold would see the Jeep approaching and when the time was right he would surface. But what if he was not there?

When he saw a dark shadow between the piles of rubble he had Poti stop the car for a moment, but the shadow was gone when he got out to investigate. However, Alex must have seen something too because he got out before Poti started up again.

He took a few steps in the opposite direction and then bent down. Karl could see that he was helping Harold to his feet. His friend walked kind of awkward and was bleeding from his head.

He answered the questioning look from Karl with a shake of his head, boarded the car and motioned to keep on going.

"What happened?" Karl asked, wiping his friends face with a rag.

"Nothing that I did not expect. It's all good, I think." In spite of the scratches on his head, Harold seemed to be in an excellent mood.

"Where were you and how did you injure your head?"

"Oh, that," Harold smiled and touched his forehead. "I slipped and fell."

"And your stumbling was also self-inflicted. But, I know, don't ask." In spite of Harold's smile Karl was worried about him.

"Look, I know that you have questions. But, first let's get out of here." Harold was eager to leave the plaza.

"You want to change back into your uniform?" Karl gestured to Poti to step on it. Harold nodded his head and after a short stop at Becker's apartment they were back at their quarters.

*****

The Kommissar was not in the building but the Belorussian Major who was Harold's language instructor was waiting for his student.

"How was your morning?" Karl greeted his father when he walked into the room.

"Nothing to complain about. They gave me plenty to eat including some excellent dried fish."

"Really?" Karl recoiled and his eyes rolled almost out of their sockets. He remembered now that his father had always liked seafood while his mother, just like Karl, abhorred it.

"Well, I am glad that you like it. I think that the Russians have plenty of it."

While Karl was discussing with his father possible strategies to find their way to the Elbe River, it occurred to him that his father could possibly manage to survive on dried fish. At least for a few days.

Come to think of it, if Alex could supply him with maybe two loaves of bread and a bunch of dried fish their food situation would be settled.

"Any idea of when we will be able to leave?" For the first time in weeks, Herr Veth was not hungry and because of this he felt great. With his uniform gone and now in somewhat fitting civilian clothing, he almost started to believe that his son could really get him to the Western Allies.

Karl shrugged his shoulders. "I don't know exactly when. Hopefully within the next two days. You taught me to allow myself to think in terms of possibilities. Let's discuss some alternatives in case we are unable to leave Berlin."

Karl's eyes wandered to the military boots his father was still wearing. "This reminds me, I got you some shoes that will go with your clothing. If they fit, they will be better for walking." He had offered his father's military boots to Herr Becker in exchange for some lighter footwear. It seemed to him that they had about the same shoe size.

He walked out to the Jeep to get them. In addition to the

shoes he had also been able to secure some socks from Herr Becker. The shoes fit almost perfect and his father was in seventh heaven. Karl took the old heavy boots and carried them back to the car.

Four

"It's about time you showed up," a booming voice greeted Harold.

"Sorry to keep you waiting, Major." He pointed to the scrapes on his head. "I ran into a wall and had to clean myself up."

"Indeed, this must be the strangest excuse I have ever heard." He motioned to Harold to join him in the courtyard of the office building. Just when he wanted to ask Harold some questions about their prior session, one of Godunov's guards, a Tatar, walked by carrying a bag filled with war souvenirs. Somehow he was not looking where he was walking and collided with a Russian soldier. His bag opened up and the loot spilled on the ground.

As he gathered the booty, the other soldier assaulted him with a barrage of grunts and snorts. They sounded to Harold like curses or invectives. Despite the fact that the Tatar was bigger and stronger then the Russian, he kept quiet and there was no visible reaction from him. He kept on picking up his belongings and when he was done he wanted to continue his walk. At this point the Russian screamed even louder. Not only this, but he also hopped up and down in front of the Tatar.

"What kind of a language is he using?" asked Harold, surprised by the stoic attitude of the Tatar. "Apparently the Tatar does not understand a word that is being hurled at him."

"He is talking in Buryat and the Tatar understands him alright. However, watch this. I will also speak Buryat to him." The Major got up and addressed the still unperturbed soldier in quiet tones. But, the more he talked the more agitated the former tranquil Tatar became. Before the Russian could retreat, the Tatar was on top of him. It was not much of a fight. The Tatar was so upset that it was no contest. He grabbed the hapless soldier by the arm and hit him with the bag mercilessly over the head until he collapsed. For good measure he added a few kicks with his boots. It was over as fast as it had begun. After grunting some more unintelligible words at the Major and offering something like a salute, the Tatar took his bag and sauntered away.

"What the heck was that? What did you tell the guy?" Harold wondered.

"There is a lesson for you, Harold." The Major sat down again. "First of all there is no real difference, other than a few limited languages, between the Tatars. In effect they are all of central Asian ancestry."

"The guard with the loot only understood Buryat and the Russian had some obviously very limited knowledge of it. For one reason or another he was jealous of the Tatar and called him a worthless piece of animal dung and human shit."

The Major smirked at Harold. "This had no effect on the Tatar because in the Buryat language you cannot insult someone by calling him names. It simply makes no sense to them."

He smiled some more. "In order to insult them you have to explain to them that you desire to insult them. So I explained to the plunderer that the Russian wished to insult him and in his mind the Tatar was stinking like a combination of human excrement and pigs manure and that the refined nostril of the Russian soldier was deeply offended by smell of it."

"Good grief," Harold looked at the Russian soldier who had slowly gotten up and limped away. "Is this the same in the Russian language?" He wanted to know.

"Oh no. You call a Russian a pig, he will deck you. No explanations are necessary. Never confuse the languages."

"Good to know,'" agreed Harold. "By the way, did the Tatar just thank you for your explanation?"

"Yes, he did," confirmed the Major. "The Mongolians are very polite, when they are sober. Now, let's get on with our regular lesson."

Harold absorbed everything the Major taught him. He was willing to learn and his mind was like a sponge. By the time the sun went down he was in command of a few helpful words and phrases.

When the Kommissar entered the courtyard Harold was able to inquire if he had experienced a pleasant day. Godunov's answer, however, escaped him.

"Don't worry," the Pompolit assured him. "You seem to have a natural talent for the Russian language. You are doing very well."

The evening was spent again in the boys' bedroom and Harold finally answered some of Karl's question.

"We know that the surrender of Berlin was on May 2nd," Harold started.

"Of course. How could I forget?" Karl wondered what his friend's statement could mean.

"We also know that some of our Wehrmacht troops tried to fight their way from the Russians, to surrender to the Western Allies and that the actual surrender of Germany occurred on May 8th," Harold continued. "Now, do you also know that some pocket guerilla forces still exist around Berlin?" he asked.

Herr Veth answered instead of Karl. "Yes, we heard of German partisan commandos. Supposedly SS and HJ units."

He looked at the boys. "When we were taken prisoner there were several rumors that they would be able to liberate us. They were supposed to hide near the railroad stations to sabotage the transport trains to Russia." He wiped his forehead. "Nothing but stupid rumors. Nobody came for us."

Karl looked at his friend with an incredible expression.

"You contacted a Werewolf unit. (Werewolf was the name for various small resistance commandos in Berlin and in certain parts of Germany after the surrender. They consisted of fanatical SS and HJ members and were mostly very ineffective.) I can see it in your eyes. Are you insane?"

"Not at all, I am just getting even," Harold answered calmly.

"Getting even, for what, with whom?" Karl really feared that his friend had lost his reasoning.

"For my mother, for one thing. With the SS for another." In contrast to Karl, Harold was not agitated at all.

"Your mother I can understand but it was not the Zampolit who raped her." While Karl was berating his friend, Herr Veth listened to the boys without understanding what the ruckus was about.

"What is it to you? Besides you should have known better than to ask. Deal with it." Harold prepared to go to bed. "One more thing, so you sleep better. I have not even begun to avenge my mother."

"Harold, I implore you, what do you mean by getting even with the SS?" Karl honestly feared for his friend. If the SS partisans found out that Harold was working for the Kommissar he would be as good as dead. And all this after they had survived the war. He had thought that they would be friends forever. But what Harold was doing now was as close to suicide as he could come.

"What do I mean? I told you not to ask but since you persist I will tell you. The Kommissar thinks I am his partner and now the SS thinks that I am their partner too. In truth, the fun has not even begun and I am enjoying myself already." Harold was on his cot and turned on his side facing the wall.

Karl didn't say another word. He knew his friend too well. He knew when to stop.

"Listen to me, Karl. Remember, I learned a lot from you. There is nothing that can go wrong. It will get interesting. Promise." Harold felt that he had to end the evening on a lighter note because he knew that Karl would worry for him. Probably all night long.

"Good night, Harold. Good night, Pappa." Karl could not think of an answer, mostly because he knew that his friend had done this for him; to get him off the hook with the Kommissar.

The next morning the hours passed swiftly. Harold resumed his lessons with the Major and Karl finally had the time to bond again with his father. He showed him the two postcards he had received from his mother during the weeks before the surrender, which were of great news to his father. They talked about Willy, Karl's 8-year-old brother and Monica his five-year-old sister, who had also added her name to the last message. After exchanging some memories the conversation returned to their primary concern; how to get out of the Russian-occupied territory.

"These shoes fit really well and I could easily walk thirty kilometers or more each day," Herr Veth assured his son.

"I am glad to hear that and I think that once we are out of the city it will be easy for us to hide. I assume that there will only be motorized patrol units and we should see them coming from far away." Karl had decided to concentrate on one part of their escape route at a time. "The real task is how to get out of the city. It seems that the individual Auffangslager (camps to catch fugitives) are still functioning. Just yesterday I saw more than three of them between the Moorenstrasse and the Uhlandstrasse. They are constantly being supplied by the roaming patrols."

"Does not sound that we will get very far without being picked up," Herr Veth agreed.

'There is however, the possibility of using the flooded subway system." Karl looked searchingly at his father. He tried to guess if his father would consider stepping in the contaminated water. "At the very least we should be able to reach the suburbs. I can't imagine that the Russians patrol the evil stinking mess."

"Didn't you say that it was flooded?"

"Yes, it is flooded but not very deep. I doubt that the water would reach our chests. It is the many corpses which are floating in it, plus the excrements and rats, which might deter the Russians. There are whole hospital trains which were flooded when the SS blew the bulk heads to the Landwehr Canal." Karl reached for a piece of bread that was left over from the morning and started to chew on it.

"Maybe some of the wounded survived but the odds were against them." He fingered the back of his neck which sometimes still bothered him. "If we decide on this route we will, however, have the additional challenge of keeping our food from getting wet and contaminated."

Karl got up and waved at his father. "Let's go down to the kitchen and search for some lunch." He sniffed the air. "Most likely it will be some cabbage soup. They always spice it with plenty of onions."

It had been an easy guess. It seemed that the whole building smelled of cabbage. Alex was already seated and greeted Karl with his usual choppy grunts. "Ka, Ka, Poodel, Ka, Ka, Poodel."

"Do you understand what he is saying?" Karl's father was amazed when his son answered with "Poodel, Poodel".

"No, I don't understand a word. His name is Alex, but for one reason or another he does not respond to it. I have to call him Ex, Ex to get his attention and he calls me Ka, Ka."

Alex had left the kitchen and came back with some pieces of moist black Russian bread. His smile spread across his entire face as he handed the bread to Karl. "Poodel, Poodel, Ka, Ka,"

"Oh, yes. He calls the bread Poodel. And he always finds some somewhere," Karl continued to explain to his father.

Herr Veth broke the bread apart. It smelled fresh and he could not figure out why it was so clammy. "I fear that this might get moldy within a day," he remarked.

The door opened and Harold stuck his head in the kitchen. "The Major will take me to the Becker's," he informed Karl. "I need the civilian clothing again. If I am not back by dark you might start searching for me."

Karl was immediately concerned. "Where are you going? Where do I search for you?"

"Herr Becker will tell you." He didn't wait for another question from his friend; he just hurried down the hallway.

No sooner was he gone before Kete came to summon Karl to the Kommissar.

"We will have to go to the victory celebration. General Berzarin expects me and my detail to arrive early. He informed me that Marshal Zhukov and several of his officers will also attend."

Godunov seemed to be in an excellent mood. His daughter had spent a peaceful night and thanks to Karl's ointment her wounds were starting to heal. He intended to keep her in hiding for the time being. If everything went in accordance with his plan, he would be able to transfer her from her present unit to a research hospital in Moscow.

"You will stay with your father and my daughter in this building. I assigned some Russian soldiers to assure your safety," he continued.

"Will there be any American or English visitors at the party?" Karl wondered if he missed a chance to meet an American officer. He was not sure how that would benefit him or his father, but in his mind he thought of all kinds of possibilities.

"Not that I know of, but I think I know what you are thinking. Don't worry, if you are taking care of my problem I will find a solution to yours." Before Godunov dismissed the boy he turned to Kete to give him some instructions.

A few minutes later Karl found himself with his father in

their regular sleeping quarters. Four Russian soldiers had arrived and split up. Two of them took positions at the door to the Kommissar's bedroom and two sat on the table chewing on some onions. Alex had been very hesitant to leave Karl and it took the Kommissar's direct order to finally get him out of the room.

"This giant is really attached to you," Karl's father observed after he was gone.

"Yes, I wonder how this will end when Godunov leaves Berlin. Alex and Kete are his primary body guards and I am sure that they will have to go with him. But, I am equally sure that Alex wants to stay with me."

Karl continued to tell his father how he had cared for Alex's feet. "The Russians treat the Tatars worse than we would treat a mangy animal, Pappa. I am sure that Alex never, ever, experienced any kindness." He finished his story and went downstairs to the restroom. One of the Russian soldiers scampered after him and he suspected this was also for his safety as the Kommissar had told him.

While father and son were deliberating all kinds of alternative ways to get to Westphalia, Karl became increasingly anxious about Harold. The last he had seen of him was when he had looked out of the window. Harold had been sitting next to his language instructor in a dilapidated Russian truck and that was several hours ago. Karl had no idea how he could possibly get away from his Russian guards in case he needed to search for his friend. To top it off, the Becker's apartment was a good thirty minute walk away.

And then what? Without a car or truck and without Alex or Kete, he could not really imagine how he would look for his friend. With every passing hour his tension mounted.

Herr Veth could not help noticing his son's nervousness. He had heard Harold's remark before the boy left and he understood Karl's anxiety.

"What do you think is causing Harold's delay?" he asked his son to show that he shared his concern.

"I don't know what to think anymore." Karl was nearly beside himself. It was getting dark and he had to get away to talk with Herr Becker.

The only thing he could think of was to escape through the

restroom window. However, he had no idea if the guards had orders to shoot. He could not imagine that the Kommissar had given any instructions to this effect, but he didn't know. All he was sure of was that his friend depended on him.

"Whatever happens, Pappa, please don't leave the room. Godunov assured me of your release and I don't think that the guards will follow me. I'll be back as soon as possible."

He got up and went out the door. To his surprise none of the soldiers followed him. When he got to the ground floor he heard a car drive up and some shouting. The front door busted open and the Kommissar came storming in followed by Alex, Kete and the rest of his guards.

He took one look at Karl and grabbed him by his coat.

"Is my daughter alright? Where do you think you are going?" he demanded.

"I need to find Harold. I'm afraid that he is in some kind of trouble."

"Trouble?" Godunov repeated. "There is trouble all over the city. Your SS Werewolf units ambushed Kozlov's convoy in Gatov and supposedly killed him. Another group tried to attack the gathering at General Berzarin's headquarters. Luckily we got tipped off. None of them survived."

He stopped himself and stared at Karl. "Did you say Harold is missing?"

Karl did not miss a beat. "Did you just tell me that Kozlov was killed?"

Godunov understood in an instant. "Take Alex and Kete with you. Go, go, go; Poti is still in the car." He yelled some commands to his guards and ran up the stairs to look after his daughter.

Karl was already sitting next to Poti when the other two Tatars joined him.

"To the Becker's!" shouted Karl and then realized that Poti did not understand him. He drove on anyhow and Karl directed him to their destination.

"Open up. It's me, Karl, open up, please." Herr Becker took a step backwards when he saw the three Tatars next to Karl.

"Come in," he wanted to wave them in, but Karl wasted no time.

"Tell me where Harold went!" he almost screamed.

PARTNERS TO A DEGREE

As Herr Becker hesitated to answer, Frau Becker spoke up from the background of the apartment. "Tell Karl what he needs to know."

A moment later Karl was back in the car, mentally repeating the information he had received.

Five

Harold's plan had been modest enough from the onset. His main personal agenda was revenge for his mother. After hearing from the Kommissar that Kozlov was responsible for the rape of countless prisoners and German women, he had decided that the Zampolit would be the first one to repay the debt. That this action would also benefit the Kommissar as well as his friend was an added bonus.

He had never been a violent boy. However, during the last few weeks he witnessed not only the brutality the SS perpetrated on their own countrymen but also the senseless rape and slaughter by the Mongolian forces. Without really thinking about it, his values had shifted. Not to the point of becoming a self-serving fanatic, but enough to accept Godunov's generous offer of adoption. He was determined to milk it for whatever it was worth.

A few days ago he had overheard Herr Becker mentioning that there were still some SS partisan groups active in Berlin. He had pressed him to reveal what he knew about them including their last known hideouts.

His strategy was simple. He had ascertained the exact location of Kozlov's headquarters and then contacted the Werewolf entity in the rear of the Anhalter station. As far as he could determine, the unit consisted of about a dozen fanatical SS members. Their armament was down to nearly nothing; a few Panzerfaust (anti-tank weapon), some explosives and some submachine guns. The goal of the Werewolfs in Berlin was to kill high ranking officers of the enemy and to fight to the last bullet. Surrender was not on their agenda.

PARTNERS TO A DEGREE

When Harold told them about the rank of the Zampolit and the route he would have to take to join the victory celebration, the Werewolf detail immediately decided to intercept him. The truck or car carrying the Zampolit would not be armored and would have to travel for a short distance along a narrow rural road. A well-aimed Panzerfaust would virtually assure success.

When Harold had left the SS cellar, he had run into a wall and almost knocked himself out. As a precaution, in case he was followed, he had instructed Karl to pick him up on the other side of the ruins of the station.

So far, so good. But Harold thought that he had heard one of the SS men make a remark with regard to another Werewolf unit proposing an assault on General Berzarin's victory party. Since he didn't want to ask the SS any direct questions, he had decided to tell his Major, the language instructor, that he had overheard some rumors that the celebration might be the target of a renegade group. The Major had acted as Harold had anticipated and tipped off the guards.

There was only one item left on Harold's list. He wanted to know details about the assault on the Zampolit and also if the Werewolf unit had suffered any losses. If there were any survivors, he planned to relay this Godunov. As soon as he went through the cellar entrance he was pinned against the wall.

"This is the boy who gave us the information about Berzarin's party." One of the SS men he had met before dragged him by his neck towards the rear and into the main cubicle of the cellar. Harold was amazed to see the elaborate set up. He had not been in this room during his first visit and noticed a small wood burning stove in a corner. Several metal field beds - folding cots - stacked on top of each other trailed along one of the walls.

A lot of blankets were stacked in an orderly fashion on top of them. "Who else have you talked with about the celebration?" Two pair of blue eyes stared at him with an intensity that made him shudder.

"No one else," he answered and looked around. Besides the two tall SS men who held him, two more men, who looked to be 20 years old, entered the room. All of them wore the dreaded black uniform but without insignias or decorations.

"We have been betrayed and ran into an ambush and no one

else but you knew that we were planning an assault." The one who held Harold by his throat was the one talking.

"You ran into an ambush in Gatov? You missed the Zampolit?" Harold could not figure out how this was possible.

"We are not talking about Gatov. Let him go Helmut, the boy gave us good information and the Russian Kommissar is already in hell." One of the younger SS men tried to intervene. "The kid never knew that we planned to attack Berzarin," he added.

"Somebody informed the Russians about us and I am not sure if it was this kid or not, but I will find out." Helmut applied more pressure to his throat and Harold was cringing and fighting for air.

"Make room," Helmut demanded and pulled Harold toward the stove. "I will show you how to make this boy talk." He said and turned to his partner.

"Put a pot of water on the stove and bring it to a boil." His attention went back to Harold and he released the pressure. Harold had gone limp and he was sputtering and coughing as he fell to the floor.

"I want to know who you talked to after you left us." His voice was low and threatening. "I will cook your hand, one finger at a time. This should help your memory."

Harold's mind was scrambled. The insufficient air supply had done a number on his brain. He could hear but could not understand what Helmut was saying. Nothing made sense to him. He passed out.

"Darn you," Helmut was getting impatient. "Bring me the pail with cold water. I want this miscarriage to feel what I am doing to him."

Someone handed him the bucket and he drenched Harold. "Now listen up, you pig. Who did you talk to?"

Harold regained his senses and shook his head. "No one." He was still unable to think clearly.

The younger SS man tried for the second time to intercede. "You are making a mistake, Helmut. The boy did us a favor."

"This is the second time you stopped me, Franz. One more word out of you and your teeth will pay the price." He looked around the room. "Anyone else want to question my actions?" He shrieked at his group and no one answered. Helmut was the tallest and the strongest of them.

"Alright then. Hold the boy up and have another container of water ready, in case he passes out again!"

He bent down to lift Harold up by his jacket when the door of the room came crashing down. To his surprise he saw a huge Mongol bearing down on him. He reached for his knife but it was too late. The Tatar grunted deeply and a whirlwind began.

Karl had followed Herr Becker's instructions, which led his group directly to the secret basement of the Werewolf. They had approached the cellar entrance in silence and then followed the loud voices.

Helmut had forgotten to post a guard. A mistake he would never make again.

No sooner had the Tatars entered the large room than they understood what was going on. Harold was still lying on the floor in a patch of water as Poti raced down to him. With a flick of his arm he had him up and leaning next to Karl on the wall. Then he simply stood with his back toward the boys, ready to tackle anyone coming his way.

Karl had followed Poti into the room and stared in sheer disbelief at the fast and brutal handiwork of Alex and Kete. He had seen the two tough men in action before, but he was not prepared for what he witnessed now.

The last time the two Tatars had been up against some Russian plunderers. They had been convincing but not lethal. This time was different. The Mongolians had recognized the black SS uniforms and were bent on killing.

Alex fought with his bare hands. He allowed Helmut to draw his knife and then reached for his hand, twisted it around with a sickening sound and pushed the knife deeply into the abdomen of the SS man. Letting go of the knife he grabbed Helmut's body and slammed him over the glowing wood stove. It sounded as if every bone in his body was being broken.

Kete had reached for the nearest partisan and crashed his head repeatedly against the metal frame of the cellar door. The SS man let out a nauseating scream and stayed down.

The third SS man was instantly out of commission when Alex got hold of an iron skillet on the stove. With a force that only a giant could release, he smashed the pan squarely into the unlucky man's face.

"No, no, no!" screamed Harold as Alex turned on Franz, the youngest of the partisans. He remembered that this fellow had spoken on his behalf. "No, not him," he pleaded as Alex crushed the nose of the young man with his elbow.

"Ex, Ex, Nooo!" yelled Karl at the top of his lungs. The giant let go of the man and looked around to face the boys. Karl could see unbridled determination in Alex's eyes and he did not dare to interfere.

"Please, Alex, spare him," Harold repeated his appeal for mercy fully aware that the Tatar did not understand a word he was saying. Or did he?

Alex looked from Harold to the SS man with the broken nose and then pushed him with a grunt to Poti who led him by his ear out of the room. Alex followed him with the two boys and only Kete stayed back for a moment to finish what they had begun.

Nobody said a word when they got into the car. Karl wanted to guide Poti back to their quarters but it seemed that the driver was determined to take a detour. When they passed a detention area for the SS, Poti stopped and addressed the Russian guards. Kete, however, was not in a mood to waste any time. He merely pushed the young SS man out of the car and motioned for Poti to drive on. Neither Harold nor Karl looked back. There was nothing either of them could do. But, they knew that Franz would live. For a while anyhow.

When they pulled into the courtyard, Alex acted as if nothing had happened and only Kete bothered to inform the Kommissar of the events. The boys walked up to their room and talked quietly with Herr Veth to bring him up to snuff while Alex stretched out on the floor as usual.

It was way past midnight when the door to their bedroom opened and one of Godunov's guards woke Karl and Harold to lead them to Godunov's office. Alex also got up and walked right behind them.

Godunov sat behind his desk and Anna, his daughter, was sitting next to him. It was the first time that the boys had a real chance to see her. Harold could detect some resemblance to the Kommissar, especially in the high forehead and the steel grey eyes. Karl, however, admired her well-fitting uniform. He thought that she looked very young for a medical officer.

"I know it is late so I'll get right to the point," Godunov begun. "We received confirmation that Zampolit Kozlov was ambushed by a Werewolf unit and was killed. I'd like to add that I am not surprised." He looked from Karl to Harold and his eyes rested for a moment longer on Harold.

"General Berzarin wishes to ship Kozlov's body to Moscow for a State funeral service but I was told that a Panzerfaust shredded his car and everyone in it. There might be not enough body parts to send home."

It appeared to Karl that the Kommissar sounded almost happy.

"I have been ordered to be present at the service and will have to leave in a day. My daughter will travel with me," he continued. "I woke you up to tell you that I will have to be with General Berzarin all day tomorrow." He looked at Harold. "I expect you to continue your language lessons with Major Tesslov. I will send for you if I am unable to return."

He shifted his eyes to Karl. "You are free to leave with your father anytime you wish. I had sincerely hoped that you would reconsider and take me up on my offer, but I understand and wish you well."

Karl was dumbfounded for a moment. The events of the last two days happened so fast and while he hoped to be finally free, he was never-the-less speechless.

He got up and the Kommissar rounded the desk to meet him halfway. He placed his arms around Karl and held him tight.

"Thank you Karl, and my daughter thanks you too. This is why she is here. I doubt that we will ever see each other again but I would like to tell you that I will never forget you." The Kommissars eyes were moist and so were Karl's. "Thank you, Herr Godunov," he stammered, unable to say anything else.

He went to shake hands with Anna who kissed him on both cheeks and pressed his hands so hard that it almost hurt.

Harold had also gotten up and hugged his friend. "I am so happy for you. I almost wish I could go with you." There were no other words between them as they would have been insufficient anyway.

Everyone was choking on their words and had tears in their

eyes.

Alex had followed the conversation without understanding a word. His eyes had never left Karl and were wide alert when the Kommissar embraced Karl. He grunted a few syllables to the Kommissar who shook his head and answered with a few of his own.

Karl was unsure what was expected of him and advanced slowly to the door.

"Can Harold go with me? I'd like to say good bye to him in private."

"Of course, Karl. But where are you going?"

Karl's breathing almost stopped. He had said *goodbye* to Godunov once before, only to be called back by the intelligence officer.

"I, I, I don't really know," he stammered. "This all happened so fast. But I will try to get to the Elbe River and to the American forces. And then to my mother."

"You plan to walk to the Elbe River? You will never make it Karl. Our military still watches for able men to send to Siberia. Where is your head?"

The Kommissar's voice was friendly enough to cause Karl to turn and face Godunov

"Do you have any suggestions, Herr Godunov?"

"This is the problem with you Germans. You will never understand the Russian soul." He reached for a letter on his desk and handed it to Karl. It was embossed with several seals.

"This is a document assuring you a safe passage, in case you get stopped. But, honestly, I cannot envision how this could happen because Alex will be with you when Poti drives you to the Elbe River and to the western forces."

For the second time that night Karl was searching for words. He could not even fully comprehend what was happening. All of his worries had disappeared in an instant. But at the very same time he also recognized the awesome authority of a senior political Kommissar. An incredibly powerful man in the forces of the Soviet Union.

"When?" He finally managed to ask.

"Poti will be ready when you are. It is barely a three-hour drive to the border and I need my men back before nightfall."

One more embrace and the boys were on their way back to their room.

"Pappa, by tomorrow night we should be with Mutti," Karl woke his father who was too startled to answer.

"Hurry up and get dressed. We leave as soon as you are ready." Karl continued to fully shake his father awake and then turned to his friend.

"I never expected this from Godunov," Karl said over and over again. "Promise me you will be extremely careful in your relationship with him. Keep your back against the wall. And...thank you for being a true friend."

Harold was also overwhelmed by the speed with which their circumstances were changing. He had to swallow hard before he could respond.

"I wish that my mother was still alive, or at least that my father was not a prisoner. I think that I would have declined Godunov's offer. But come what may, we will always be friends." He swallowed again. "Thanks for showing up with Alex and the others when the chips were down."

"Oh, that was nothing compared to your ingenuity with the Kozlov challenge. How do we stay in contact?" Karl was eager to end the sentimentalities and use the final few minutes constructively.

"Well, you know my intentions. I don't know where they will take me but, I will always aim to return to Berlin. Let's use the Becker family as an exchange of information." Harold tried to think of a fall-back contact. However, nothing came to mind.

It was as if Karl was reading his friend's mind. "We might need a secondary method, but I agree that this is the only viable option at this time. I will stop by the Becker's on my way out and say goodbye."

Harold looked over to Alex who had received his orders from the Kommissar and stood solemnly at the door, ready to go.

"What about him?"

"Yes, Harold, you are right. What about him? I will more than miss the brutal but good-hearted giant. Please try to look after him; if you can."

"You got it, Karl. I promise."

Karl gathered his few pieces of clothing and the boys went

down to the car. Herr Veth was already sitting on the bench in the back of the Jeep.

Both boys tried to keep their emotions in check. It was a joyful and at the same time bitter moment in their lives. A moment they never forgot.

Harold was stepping back when Karl sat down next to Poti.

"You lucky dog," he smiled under tears.

"Thank you, Harold. Yes, I am a lucky dog." He wanted to follow his friend's example and smile. But, the more he tried, the harder it got. He could not do it.

Six

It was already close to three in the morning when Karl knocked on the door of the Becker's apartment.

"I have been released by the Kommissar. If everything goes well I will see my mother within a few days," he said in a way of greeting and explaining the night visit.

While he introduced his father to the Beckers, Alex proceeded to unpack two small flags which he mounted with the help of Herr Becker on the fenders of the Jeep.

The flags featured the Soviet red star and the emblem of the political Kommissar. They designated the Jeep as an official car of Kommissar Godunov. Karl wondered if Alex knew this or intended it. He looked at the standards with some apprehension. Since he could not communicate with Alex or Poti about this issue, he hoped for the best.

"We hate to see you leave, Karl, but, we are truly happy for you." Frau Becker attempted to add a cheerful note.

"I'll be back as soon as the Allies allow us to travel. In the meantime please keep any of Harold's messages for me." Karl strained to keep the sentimentalities to a minimum because he could see that Frau Becker was close to tears. Both of them realized how close they had become during the last month.

"We have to get going." He pointed at Poti who had started the car and anxiously waited for his passengers.

After a last wave, Karl directed Poti to the main thoroughfare leading out of the city. During the first hour they made hardly any progress because the road was heavily congested with an endless stream of American vehicles entering Berlin.

Once they cleared the suburbs it went a little faster. Instead of claiming the whole width of the road like they did in the city, the British and American trucks kept more to the eastbound lane allowing the westbound Jeep to pass them at a greater speed.

This changed again as they came closer to the city of Magdeburg on the Elbe river. They were nearing the western territory.

In spite of Poti leaning his elbow on the horn, their progress was again slowed. This time it was a traffic mess caused by Russian troop carriers filled with POWs. The western Allied troops were traveling east, towards Berlin, and the Russian convoy tried to cross the road in a northerly direction. They were apparently bound to some railroad station by Stettin to unload their prisoners.

As every vehicle came to a complete standstill a multilingual shouting match ensued. A British military police officer was joined by an American MP who then tried to outdo each other by yelling at the Soviet truck drivers. Their effort left no impression on the Russians who didn't move a single inch out of the way.

They decided to wait for their own military police and began to chew on dried fish. Karl was surprised by Alex's civil behavior as he leaned back in his seat searching for a more comfortable position. It seemed as if the giant didn't give a hoot one way or the other until a Soviet major appeared out of nowhere.

Alex had waited for this to happen. He jumped out of the car and approached the officer who didn't pay any attention to him. He was too busy listening to his truck drivers and their complaints.

Herr Veth, who had never seen Alex in action, was astonished by what happened next.

Before the Russian major realized what was happening to him, Alex lifted him up and carried him to the front of the Jeep. Pointing at the flags of the Kommissar and motioning to Poti to speak up, he kept the officer in a vice grip forcing him to listen.

Poti, who spoke Russian, tried to explain the urgency of their mission without any visible results. The major stared with a frozen expression at the flags. He blinked a few times but did not dare to move.

Nothing had changed in the gridlock with the exception of Alex planting the Russian major on the hood of the Jeep.

Herr Veth looked questionably at Karl.

"I am afraid that it will turn ugly before we start moving again." Karl shrugged his shoulders. "I don't see the Americans moving and Alex will not release the major until he gets his way."

"What's going on? Release the major and assume position, you ape." The new voice belonged to an American officer. His name tag identified him as Captain Walker. He had arrived from the far side of the Western Allies' convoy and spoke very good Russian.

Alex was not impressed. How could he be? He only understood Buryat. Moreover, he was having fun. He hated Russian officers with a passion and he enjoyed any opportunity to demonstrate that he was not subject to their orders.

Poti, who knew Alex's nature better than anyone, did his best to sort things out between the major and the American captain. Somehow he succeeded. Walker understood that the Russian jeep carried important passengers under the protection of a high ranking Soviet political Kommissar. He motioned once more to Alex to let go of the Russian officer. Alex complied, but only after he severely tweaked the nose of the major who shrieked like a pig. He jumped down from the hood and without looking back the officer disappeared between the Russian trucks.

Captain Walker shook his head. He had heard that the Soviet political officers were the overriding authority in the Russian armies but he had never witnessed anything like this. The burly Tatar didn't even wear an officer's uniform. He figured that it must have been the star emblem on Alex's jacket which rendered the major helpless.

Poti followed Captain Walker's directions and drove the jeep across a field to a secondary road. While he waited for the Captain to follow up with further instructions, Karl compared a lonely road sign with the map he had obtained from Herr Becker.

The map showed that this road would bypass the city of Magdeburg and cross the Elbe River a few more miles upstream.

"Look at this, Pappa. Do you think that we should try this bridge?" Herr Veth took a look at the map and shook his head. "No, I don't think so. If it was operational we would see Allied vehicles coming this way."

The map showed that they were within ten miles or so from the River and Herr Veth voiced a different idea. "What do you think of trying to find a boat or some kind of a float to cross the river instead of searching for a bridge?"

"Let's keep that in mind, just in case that everything else fails." Karl had faith in Godunov's document to get them safely into western territory. He looked back and saw Captain Walker's car coming up behind them. "Maybe the driver speaks German," he speculated and walked over to the mud-covered car.

The driver, a sergeant with the name of Friedman, listened together with the Captain at Karl's attempt to communicate with them. Neither one spoke the language but they seemed interested in helping. After several minutes it looked like Poti's explanations made some sense to the Captain.

He gathered that the Russian Jeep wanted no more than to safely deliver the passengers across the river and then to return to Berlin. As far as he knew there was no official border crossing. There were only a handful of points where the Soviets allowed Allied vehicles to proceed to Berlin; otherwise, there was not much cooperation between their respective forces. The Western troops were deeply suspicious of the Russians and did not allow any Soviet vehicles to enter their territory.

The Russians had similar orders. They didn't like their American counterparts one bit. The Soviet troops had marched and fought for hundreds of miles for every single inch of German soil. Their soldiers were nearly starved and had suffered tremendous losses capturing Berlin while it was obvious that the Western Allies were well motorized and sported far superior weapons.

To top it off, it was evident that the American forces had plenty to eat and apparently never suffered from hunger. While the Russians gnawed on dried fish, plain bread and an occasional helping of cabbage soup, the Western troops seemed to have an unlimited amount of canned food.

All this was very logical to Captain Walker. He just hoped that the distrust would not spill over in a bloodbath. In his opinion all the initial fighting forces, the Western Allies as well as the Soviets, should be replaced as soon as possible with well-rested occupation troops. He also had explicit instructions to foster good will with any Soviets he encountered. The present situation looked like a good opportunity.

Upon his orders, the sergeant laid a blanket on the hood of their car and the Americans spread an unbelievable amount of goodies on top of it. Neither Alex nor Poti had ever seen such a variety of food. Corned beef and spam was something totally unknown to them and now each of them had a can of their own. Karl and Herr Veth also received their fair share and enjoyed the delicacies.

For the ensuing fifteen minutes there was no tension between them. Food is a great equalizer between hungry people.

After the meal, Friedman produced a pack of 'Camel' cigarettes and motioned to the Tatars to keep them. He even offered some to Herr Veth and Karl but both of them refused. Karl preferred to have another potato chip. He had never seen chips before and didn't know what it was he was eating.

Walker had made up his mind to guide the Russians to the border crossing where he himself had entered the Russian territory this morning. He trusted that his commanding officer would approve of his actions.

An hour later Karl and Herr Veth were interviewed by an American major. He kept Godunov's letter and told them in German that they were free to go wherever they wished in western Germany. The check point office had even provided them with two passenger certificates which allowed them to use any operating railroad line all the way to their destination in Westphalia. Most of the major railroad lines were still down, however, a few secondary lines operated without a regular schedule. They served to shuffle the ever increasing amount of refugees from the Russian zone to the inland of western Germany.

The time had come for Karl to say good bye to Alex. He had dreaded this moment throughout the whole morning. He knew that there was no way around it but he was very ill prepared.

The Tatar looked at him with wide open eyes and it seemed to Karl as if Alex's soul was in them, bare and open. He was unable to look away from the eyes which conveyed nothing but unlimited trust. For an instant Karl realized that everything in life comes with a price. And the price of seeing his mother again was saying good bye to his friends. Friends like Harold and Alex. Friends he had depended on with his life.

Herr Veth could feel the emotions his son was going through and gently tugged on his arm to hint that they should be going. Karl understood. He embraced Alex and then Poti. All three of them felt the same unspoken bond between them and hated to let go.

It took Poti several attempts to get Alex back into the Jeep. For a moment it looked as if the friendly giant had a change of heart and wanted to follow the two Germans, who waved a last good bye as they walked away toward the train station.

"Darn it," said Karl as he wiped the tears from his eyes. "It looks like my whole life is nothing but a parade of endless farewells and I am not very good at it." He looked helplessly at his father.

"I agree that you had your share of it, but now you also have something to look forward to. In another day you will see your mother and your brother and sister again." Herr Veth admired his son for having the honesty to admit his feelings.

The local railroad station was packed with refugees and it appeared that no one had a definite destination in mind. As soon as an empty train, coming from the west, turned around to go back, it was stormed. Regardless if the announced destination was Hanover (straight to the west) or Frankfurt (more to the southwest) the mob surged toward the empty wagons to get away from the Russian territory.

To Herr Veth's relief there were just as many able men as well as women and children among the refugees. He didn't see a single American or British soldier arresting anyone. He finally realized that he was truly free. The difference of treatment between the Soviet forces and the Western Allies was almost too much to fully comprehend.

It was at this train station that Karl witnessed again the total disregard of the German adults towards unattended children. It did not matter how old the child was; if it was alone and in the way of an adult, it was brutally pushed aside and in many instances just thrown off the wagons. It reminded him of the air raid bunkers in Berlin where everyone was only thinking of themselves. But, the war was over and Karl had hoped that civilized behavior would be the norm again.

"Is there any way we could assist the children?" Karl had helped some of the homeless children in Berlin find shelter with adults and he wondered why there was no organization like a church that cared for them.

His father looked across the tumult and shook his head. "No Karl, there is nothing we can do. There are just too many of them. I am sure that in due time the German Red Cross will be active and help them."

Karl, who loved his father and wanted to believe him, was not too sure that this would happen anytime soon. But, he also realized that his father was right. It would take an organized effort to stop the madness. And, again, his inner values shifted a small degree.

Whatever respect he had left for adults faded slowly away.

It was nearly dark when Karl and Herr Veth managed to get on a train. It was standing room only and the smell of sweat and urine permeated throughout. When the train left the station a rousing shout emerged. Everyone was cheering and in spite of being hungry, food was not on anybody's mind. No one asked or knew the destination. All they knew for sure was that the wheels carried them westward, away from the Soviets.

It turned out to be an agonizingly slow trip. The train stopped often for long periods of time and when it rolled it was not very fast. By the time morning came they had traveled less than a hundred miles and everyone was hungry. Karl still had some dried fish and bread in his pockets. It was not much but it was better than nothing.

Herr Veth, who knew a little about the general route they had to take to reach Detmold, was sure that they were traveling too far to the southwest. He suggested getting off the train at the next station.

Luckily he had been right. They were in a town named Altenbeken. A place they had never heard of in Berlin. Karl and his father were the only people getting off the train and were genuinely surprised by the friendly attitude of the station master. He told them that there was no operational connection to Detmold and took them with a horse carriage to a farmer who fed them and offered to let them rest for a day.

During the following two days they walked and sometimes hitchhiked on horse-drawn ranch wagons. During the long walk, Karl told his father about his experiences with Kommissar Godunov and of Harold's reason to accept Godunov's offer of adoption.

Herr Veth kept mostly quiet and Karl reasoned that his father must have had some experiences he didn't feel like sharing. He hoped that this was only a temporary state between them because he had always liked and enjoyed when his father had answered his questions.

At night they slept in hay barns and on the third day they reached the farm where Frau Veth was staying with a distant relative.

Karl was the first one to spot his small five-year-old sister. "Monika, look over here, see who is coming," he shouted to his father's surprise across the street. The little girl looked up not sure who had called her and instead of running up to him as he had hoped, she turned and ran into a house calling for her mother.

It was a tearful but happy reunion. Frau Veth had never stopped believing that her husband was alive. The last time she had heard from him was a short letter and this was still during the war, several months ago.

She had heard that the Soviets were shipping all their POWs to Siberia and she had hoped that her husband would be exempt because of his severely limited eyesight. Herr Veth was 90 % legally blind in his left eye and the right eye was also diminished by something like 35 %. His impaired eyesight had also been the reason that he was never drafted into the regular Wehrmacht. Only Hitler's fanatical wish to leave no survivors had forced civilians like Herr Veth into the last call to arms, the Volkssturm.

Karl received a huge hug from his mother who promised to listen to his stories later. He understood and gave his parents some time for themselves and talked to his eight-year-old brother and his little sister for the remainder of the day.

The following days were filled with exchanging stories and memories. While his parents were discussing possible plans for the future, Karl felt strangely alone. Sure, he was with his parents and his siblings and he loved them dearly. Still, something didn't feel right and he could not put his finger on what it was that bothered him.

His parents assured him that it was a normal reaction after nearly two years of partial separations and reunions and that everything would turn out alright, now that the war was over. But Karl felt that it was far more than that.

For one thing, he missed his grandfather who had been arrested by the SS, never to be seen again. And he would also never again see the other few adults he had admired and trusted. Some of them had been killed and others had committed suicide to avoid responsibilities. Years ago he had asked his father and grandfather why there was a war. The answers he had received were explanatory but not sufficient to justify the suffering he had witnessed.

To make it more confusing, he did not understand the boys he met in his new surroundings. They had never experienced a single air raid or had heard a shot being fired. They had lived in Germany alright, but they had experienced a different war than he had seen.

He was now almost fifteen years old and on the train his father had told him that it was high time to decide how he wanted to earn a living. High school or college to pursue his initial choice of a legal career was clearly not an option anymore.

Herr Veth was without a job and unable to pay for any kind of higher education. Besides, there were all the wounded soldiers coming home and due to their injuries there would be a shortage of able bodied craftsmen.

Karl decided to look for a master where he could learn a trade and work as an apprentice. Under the present conditions this meant working for three years without wages except for room and board. After the three years he would be eligible to apply for a test qualifying him to become a journeyman. After an additional five years as a journeyman he could apply for the test to obtain the 'master' designation.

The real challenge was to find a master who was willing to teach him. There were not too many around. The German male population had been diminished by a great percentage.

"May I please stay for another two weeks with you?" Karl asked his parents after a few days on the farm and the initial joy of their reunion had ebbed away.

"Two weeks are alright, but then you need to decide. Your birthday is only two months away and once you are fifteen you are too old. No master will want to teach you anything."

Herr Veth was a little dismayed that Karl was still not sure how he wanted to earn a living. But he also wanted to be lenient and blamed the last months of the war for his son's indecision.

"I understand that I need to earn my keep," Karl dared to answer his father, hoping he could ask a few questions. Herr Veth nodded to his son to go on.

"I am also told that once I decide on a trade I have to live with this decision for the rest of my life." This was the real thing that Karl didn't understand.

"Let's say that I decide to become a tailor but after ten years in the trade I don't like it anymore and wish to become a butcher. Is there any law that prevents me from changing my occupation?"

There, he had asked the question which had prevented him from making a 'Berufswahl' (occupation decision). He knew that boys his age had to make this decision, but no one had told him what would happen if he had a change of heart later on in life.

At first it seemed that Herr Veth was about to explode in a sudden burst of anger. To be questioned about something so elementary and self-understood was enough to get his dander up. But then he remembered that his son had been more or less on his own during the past year and that he had earned the right to ask a question about something he did not understood.

"Well, when I was fourteen years old I knew like everyone else how I wanted to earn a living. But, Hitler and this war changed so many old tried and true values. Maybe you are right to question traditions." Herr Veth got up from the chair in the tiny room in the farm house. "Let's go out and sit in the sun for a while," he suggested.

Karl was encouraged and happy that his father actually had some time for him.

"No, there is no law against changing your mind. But you need to know what will happen and how you will be judged should you wish to change your occupation." Herr Veth sat down on a tree stump while Karl sat on the ground looking up at his father.

"Keep in mind that we are talking about trade guilds and their long-time established rules. We are not talking about the academic professions. We are also not talking about common laborers."

Herr Veth adjusted his glasses to take a better look at his son.

"If you choose to be a laborer, you will be seen as a drifter. Your choice will allow you to change from a sewage worker to a ditch digger anytime you wish. But you will be seen as a good-for-nothing tramp."

"However, if you choose a trade you will be a very much respected citizen. The first requirement is finding a master in the given trade who is a respected member of the trade guild."

He adjusted his glasses again to lock eyes with his son.

"Here comes the rub, Karl. If you wish to change to a different trade later on in life, you will never find a master who would be willing to teach you. No Master in good standing within a trade guild would ever consider teaching someone who does not know what he wants. First you choose to be a tailor and then later on you wish to become a butcher? Think about it, Karl. You would be considered as flimsy, someone who does not know what he wants. You would be even considered mentally unbalanced. Believe me, you could search for a lifetime but you would never find a master willing to teach a mentally handicapped person. Why should he? There are plenty of psychologically sound boys applying to be taught."

Herr Veth stopped his long lecture and hoped that Karl understood the full scope of what he was saying. He looked at the small farm yard searching his mind for another example.

But Karl understood. He knew that there was a real stigma against unskilled people in Germany. If he wished to succeed in life he had to decide on the trade he wanted to learn. Moreover, he had to decide on it within the next two weeks.

His mind wandered to Harold and for a second he envied him. But only for a second. He would never consider serving in the Soviet forces and he had to work hard to break his train of thought because he missed his friend. He hoped with all his heart that Harold was doing alright.

"Thank you Pappa for your advice. I will do my best to find a master within the next few days."

He decided to walk to the next town and find out if there was a headquarters or something like it for the different trade leagues. Maybe he could talk to some of the old and retired masters to get some practical suggestions. Somehow he liked the idea of becoming a toolmaker. But he also thought of becoming an automobile mechanic. Maybe he could apply for an apprenticeship in a nearby city. But first, he wanted to talk to someone who had a lifetime of experience in the given trade.

The next night he had a terrible time collecting his thoughts into a productive order. He realized why he was so down-hearted. It must be the sudden absence of an important goal, he reasoned with himself. While he had been a sub-leader in the children evacuation camps, he was responsible for the welfare of the children. While he was sharing the last weeks of the war with Harold, there had been nothing but survival on their minds. When he was performing tasks for Kommissar Godunov, he was at the same time searching for his parents.

But now? Everything was accomplished and in summation it didn't seem much. Sure, he had survived the war and found his family, but they were poor refugees among millions of others.

In all reality he now had only two weeks to enjoy his family and then he was out and on his own again. However, this time without a friend and without an urgent purpose. It was not that he was afraid of the future. No. He had proven to himself that he could handle whatever life decided to hand him. It was just the realization that growing older was a constant struggle. Maybe the firm hand of a master teacher was what he really needed.

Right then and there in the early morning hour, he decided that he would give his all to become proficient in his chosen trade.

Seven

Harold waved until he lost sight of the departing Jeep and then he needed all his strength to walk up to the empty room. It was still the middle of the night and he tried to find some sleep. When this didn't work, he reached for a sheet of paper to write a second letter to his father. He wanted the letter to be cheerful but could not think of a happy sentence.

His thoughts circled around the last few days and he finally gave up fighting his tears. However, by the time morning rolled around he was in full control of himself again.

"Good morning," Major Tesslov said as he entered the mess room. He was wearing a heavy coat and handed a thick uniform jacket and something resembling a backpack to Harold.

"We will spend the next few days on the road," he announced. "If you have any belongings make them fit in this satchel. I doubt that we will return to this place."

"Where are we going, Herr Tesslov?" Harold was happy to leave this room and the building behind. Any kind of a trip would surely distract him enough from his self-pity.

"It depends on where and how soon we are supposed to catch up with the Kommissar." Major Tesslov was happy and content with his assignment to tutor Harold. The boy was bright, a willing student and a fast learner.

It also gave him a chance to keep on repaying a huge favor he owned the Kommissar. He knew Godunov since they had studied together in Moscow. While Tesslov was strictly a military officer, fluent in a few Slavic languages and bent on learning

German, French and English, Godunov was already entrenched in a political career. This was many years ago when both officers studied together as young lieutenants. It was also before Tesslov had been tempted to fool around with the young and attractive wife of a senior officer. This in itself was not so uncommon in Moscow. Most of the senior soldiers of rank had young wives which in return had an eye for the strapping young officers in the elite schools. Tesslov had been either stupid or in puppy lust, but either way he got caught and found guilty of a civil crime against his fellow officers.

He was already condemned to a forced labor camp in the Ural Mountains when Godunov found out about it and intervened on Tesslov's behalf. Thanks to the influence of his stepfather, Godunov had advanced to the status of a junior Kommissar and it was actually his first attempt to indebt an officer to him. He did not share his plans for political advancement with anyone but they included indebting various individuals to secure his ambitions.

In some cases it had not worked out as smoothly as he had hoped. He had to turn the situation around and use his rising power to wipe out any possible trace of his attempts.

When Godunov had heard of Tesslov's transgressions and of his conviction, he had approached the NKVD (Communist secret state police) bureau in Moscow with an ingenious proposal.

He offered to 'lease' the language wizard from the labor camp under the pretense that he needed him for intelligence work during the war. He vouched for Tesslov with his name and signed a document that he would return him to the prison when he no longer needed him. In the meantime, he sent two other criminals to the camp to serve as replacement for Tesslov. Nobody assumed he had an ulterior motive or questioned him about his actions.

He personally picked up Tesslov from the central prison in Moscow and when they reached his office he showed him the obligation he had signed. Tesslov understood that he was free as long as he served Godunov's interests. Before his conviction he had reached the rank of a major and now it was impossible for him to advance any further. However, from time to time, Godunov rewarded him with certain perks. Mostly recommendations for medals. It was an unspoken painless agreement between them and Godunov liked the simplicity of it.

PARTNERS TO A DEGREE

The more Tesslov thought about his present task the more he liked it. Godunov had not only ordered him to teach Harold the Russian language on a fast track, but he was also to test the intelligence level of his protégé. He was supposed to immerse Harold in challenging situations and observe the boy's ability to handle himself. Tesslov, on the other hand, figured if he played his cards right he might find, with the unwitting help of the boy, a weak spot in the Kommissar's armor. He was looking for anything that might level the playing field. It was not that he didn't feel thankful and grateful towards Godunov, but he wanted to be on even terms and not at his mercy. In spite of his pending prison term, he had some plans for himself.

*****

Harold had only a few items of clothing which he fitted neatly in the backpack and then he followed the Major to a newly seized American-built four-wheel-drive vehicle. It easily seated six people and was painted in the Russian camouflage colors with a bright red Soviet star. The appropriation from a supply convoy from the Baltic Sea had been one of the latest actions by the Kommissar before he had left with his bodyguards to join the city commander Berzarin.

"Do you know where the prison in Spandau is located?" Tesslov asked Harold who was immediately interested.

"Yes, I was there a few days ago with Karl. What do you have in mind?"

"I understand that this is where your father is being held. Maybe there is a chance that you can see him before we leave Germany." Tesslov had no plan or any idea of how to do this, but he wanted to give an appearance of sympathy. He hoped that this would earn him points with the boy.

Harold showed the way out of the city but was only cautiously hopeful. He remembered Godunov telling him that there was no chance, even for a political Kommissar, to assure his father's freedom. Still, Tesslov's suggestion gave him hope that they might be able to see his father. Just a simple glimpse of him would be wonderful.

The road to Spandau was again crowded with British and American vehicles but the prison itself seemed less guarded than a week ago. The multi-national guards on duty consisted of smaller groups made up by regular soldiers and not of junior officers as before.

Harold mentioned the reduction of guards to Tesslov who considered his possible options. He thought about how he could possibly get all four of the different nationalities on the same page, knowing that he could not bribe them as they all seemed well fed and content.

"Let's try begging." Tesslov smiled at the boy as he drove up to the guard shack and asked for the officer on duty. Within a minute they were standing in front of a broad-shouldered American first lieutenant.

The Major introduced himself as an aide to political Kommissar Godunov of the NKVD and added that the Kommissar would consider it a personal favor if his German protégé could possibly have a chance to see his father who was supposedly detained in this facility.

Lieutenant Logan listened with respect to the flawless English of the Russian officer and shook his head. "Sorry Major, but I have no choice in the matter. No one is permitted to see the political prisoners. I would happily oblige the wishes of the Kommissar if it was a matter of simply seeing a regular POW."

Tesslov shifted his eyes to Harold. "You cannot say that I did not try," he told him in German.

Harold had listened to the short discussion with his limited understanding of the English language and thought he had heard something that might be worthwhile following up on.

"My father is not a political criminal. If he is here at all it must be by mistake." His English was far from perfect but the American understood the meaning and felt sorry for the German boy in the unfitting Russian uniform.

"I am not the one who decides whether a prisoner is a war criminal or not." Logan turned to a wall cabinet and retrieved a list of names. "Most of the detainees have been shipped to Luxembourg for interrogation before their trial," he informed the Major.

"What is your father's name and rank?" he asked Harold.

"My father's name is Ferdinand Kellner and he had no rank. He was a civil employee in charge of supplies."

The lieutenant took a second look at the boy before he consulted his list. "Let me give you some advice. Never, ever, say that your father was in charge of anything. Civil employee is good enough." His eyes returned to the paper in his hand. "I will forget what I heard," he spoke to no one in particular.

Harold understood immediately. Karl had always told him that he talked too much. Now he somehow received the same advice from an American officer. *Time to pay attention*, he told himself.

"Your father's name is not on this list," Lieutenant Logan told Harold without saying what kind of list it was.

"It could be that Herr Ferdinand Kellner is only guilty by association. If this is the case, he might still be in this facility waiting to be assigned to a different prison," Logan informed the major. "As I stated before, I want to be helpful to the Kommissar and to this boy, but I need to first consult with the prison commander. Please wait." Without saying how long this might take he left the guard office.

A few minutes passed and when he returned he was smiling. "Follow me." He motioned to Harold and Tesslov to accompany him into the prison yard which had several sections separated with barbed wire.

"You will have five minutes with your father. It is all I could do for you."

Herr Ferdinand Kellner appeared from a back building followed by a prison guard in a British uniform. He did not recognize his son until he was within shouting distance. In the next moment they were both holding each other, searching for words.

Lieutenant Logan pretended to look at his watch but in reality he allowed the reunion to last at least twice as long as permitted.

"Say your goodbye and tell your father that he is a lucky man to have a determined son like you." The lieutenant ended the short visit. Harold embraced his father once more and followed him with his eyes until he disappeared into the far building.

"Do you know what might happen to my father? You said something like *'guilty by association'* what does this mean?" Harold asked Logan wiping the joyful tears from his eyes.

"All I know is that your father is not one of the officially named war criminals. But, he might belong to a group that will be judged as criminals during the upcoming trial. If that happens he might be sentenced to a prison term."

The American Lieutenant glanced at the Russian Major before he continued. "In any event it would be a much better fate than being forced into slave labor in Russia."

They were walking back towards the guardhouse and Tesslov took the stab at the Russian practice of sending their prisoners to Russia with remarkable ease.

"Tell me, Lieutenant, where are you from, in the USA?"

"Virginia."

"I always liked that name and I heard that Virginia is a great state with many tobacco plantations. But tell me how many cities in Virginia have been destroyed by the Germans? How many roads or utility or railroad lines have been devastated enough to push you back almost to the Middle Ages? And finally, how many lives including women and children have the Americans lost compared to the millions my country has lost?"

When the Lieutenant hesitated a moment too long to respond, Tesslov stretched out his hand to Logan. "Don't bother to answer, Lieutenant, we have to thank you for helping us, but don't condemn us for wanting the people who devastated our country to rebuild it again. We never invited the Germans to invade us and we are simple people calling it tit-for-tat."

The Lieutenant hesitated before he shook Tesslov's hand. "I agree that you have a valid point, Major. Without our material help you would still be fighting around the Volga River. And don't forget our Air Force, and……" he hesitated again, "well, forget it. It's over."

"Interesting American slang, I take it. You Americans say forget it and get on with your business. We Russians can't even comprehend this phrase as we will never forget. I wish you well on your return home." Tesslov let go of the Lieutenant's hand and turned around to leave when he heard Logan's answer. "Same to you, Major." He slowly turned his head to take another look at the American. "I wish I had a home to go home to."

Harold had followed the conversation between the officers with some discomfort. While he was still happy to have seen and spoken with his father, he was also aware that the Lieutenant was no match against his Major. It bothered him that the Russian was essentially correct in his answers. He decided to come back to this subject and discuss it with Godunov when he saw him again.

For now, he was more than thankful that Tesslov had helped him. He had never expected to see his father today. "If there is ever anything I can do for you, please tell me." He was bent on repaying Tesslov for the favor.

"I am not an American, so I won't tell you to forget it. We will spend a long time together and I am sure that there will be many opportunities in our future to assist each other."

The Major was very satisfied with how the day had turned out. He was a bit sentimental himself and enjoyed seeing Harold so happy. This alone was worth the afternoon, but he was also pleased to hear Harold's assurance.

"We will stay tonight in the castle of Genshagen," he announced as he turned the car back on the road. "Do you know the fastest route?"

Harold had to interrupt his thoughts because his mind was still with his father. But then he remembered that the castle was near Ludwigsfelde, Brandenburg, and this was the place where the highly placed German civil servants had been evacuated by the German high command and then had subsequently been arrested by the Russians.

This was also the place where the Kommissar had found his mother. Maybe this would be an opportunity to find some information in regard to the specific unit that had been involved with the mass rape that caused his mother's death. He struggled with some ideas as to how he could use the Major for this purpose.

"I am not too sure, Herr Tesslov. I don't know of a direct route. The fastest way would be to cross the outskirts of Berlin." The dilapidated map he consulted showed no major thoroughfare to the south. He looked at the traffic going in their direction and noted the total absence of any American or British troops.

Kind of strange, he mumbled to himself. "What is strange?" The Major had heard him and thought that Harold's remark was related to their destination.

Harold caught himself short and steered the conversation in the direction of his foremost interests. "Could you please observe and correct me tonight? I would like to try and apply what you taught me with some of the soldiers we will meet."

"Yes, this is a very good idea. There will be soldiers from different parts of Russia. If nothing else you will learn how to differentiate between the dialects."

The Major was happy to see Harold's eagerness. He reasoned that his enthusiasm was due to the successful visit they just had.

Eight

They reached the castle shortly before dark. It was an imposing, huge building with no real visible damage and Harold strained his memory to recall the history of this place. It must not have been too important because nothing came to mind. He marveled at the impressive doors and the ornamentation around the windows.

The large structure was surrounded by something like a park, however at the present time it looked more like an oversized parking lot for military vehicles.

Major Tesslov feared that some high-ranking officer would notice his four-wheel-drive and claim the almost new car for himself. He could contest this action and his credentials might win the day, but he was not about to take any chances. He had no personal bodyguards and decided to drive his car all the way down and around a long hedge to partially hide it.

While the building was occupied by Ukrainian forces it was also partially under the command of Belarusian troops and there was no pretense of love between them. If anything, they would steal from each other. This had been true as long as Tesslov could think back. But now, after the Tatar shock troops of the Ukrainian forces had suffered incredible losses during the battle of Berlin, it was the Belarusians who demanded their part, if not most, of the plunder.

Marshal Zhukov had been fully aware of this conflict and in order to prevent a drawn-out bloodbath between his troops he solved the problem in a unique way. A few days after the Tatars had been ordered home, his Belarusian troops "accidentally" rolled their tanks over some of the Mongolian units who were "kind of slow" in following orders. Neither Kommissar Godunov nor Major Tesslov, both of them Ukrainian by birth, had been surprised by this unfortunate incident. After all, the Tatars were not eager to go anywhere. They had been promised the spoils of war. They had fought and died for the rewards of a winning army and the survivors had no home to go back to.

The general idea had been to ship the Mongols to central Asia, the place of their ancestors, but they had been nomads and homeless to begin with. Most of them had been recruited on the Crimean Peninsula and the Soviet Army was essentially their home. Furthermore, their tremendous fatalities had diminished their structured units to practically nothing. So after the initial few shock troop trains had left Berlin for destinations unknown, it was considered to be good enough.

The high command reckoned it would be more productive to use the trains to ship POWs to the east. They had also officially announced that there was no conflict between their troops, figuring if there was... it would eventually sort itself out.

These conditions had turned into something like a "free for all" whenever the plentiful free-flowing Vodka encouraged the participants.

*****

"Since when has your regiment occupied this castle?" Harold looked for a side door. He saw an argument developing at the main entrance.

"I don't know. I was temporarily attached to the city commander. This is my first time here and we will leave tomorrow morning." The Major was not intimidated by the squabble and walked confidently next to another Ukrainian officer towards the entry hall.

It looked like the quarrel was caused by a Ukrainian lieutenant who tried to pass the doorway with two women at his side. He would have been successful if not for a few Belarusian soldiers who tried to talk him out of his intentions.

While they were arguing, Tesslov grabbed one of the girls by the waist - it was the younger one, Harold noticed- and kept on walking towards a staircase. The unknown officer next to him reached for the older girl and pushed the Lieutenant out of his way towards the soldiers who looked kind of dumbfounded at the officers and the disappearing women. It looked to Harold as if the Ukrainians acted in concert and had this done before. He hurried to keep up with his Major and lost sight of the other couple. Based upon the verbal exchange of the girls he was sure that they were not Germans. However, whether or not they were unwilling participants was not so clear. In spite of their lamenting they seemed to be content to go along.

The Major walked up to the first floor, opened a door and ordered the single occupant out of the room.

"Find yourself something to eat and give me an hour. I need a break," he announced to Harold, pushing the girl into the chamber and closing the door behind him.

Harold was stunned to find himself alone all of a sudden among the Russians. At first he felt like sitting down in front of the door but then decided that he was not a dog. He looked towards the staircase and saw two soldiers coming his way. His first impulse was to duck and scramble out of the way when he remembered a final bit of advice from Karl. *'When all else fails, act drunk'*. He pushed himself away from the door and incoherently mumbled the few Russian curse words he had picked up. As he stumbled in his oversized Russian coat from wall to wall, the soldiers parted to give him plenty of room.

Interesting, he thought to himself. *These guys respect a drunk. Maybe it's best to keep on imitating one.* He knew the word for food and decided to use it in his ramblings. It took only a few minutes of cussing and awkward moves until a drunken Belarusian took mercy on him and guided him towards a buffet-like serving table. It didn't feature much of a selection but there were some edibles other than the ever present cabbage soup and dried fish. He was just about to load up a plate with grilled onions when someone touched him on his shoulder. He turned and looked into the grey shimmering eyes of an older Ukrainian captain. He felt as if the eyes paralyzed him.

"So, you are the understudy of Kommissar Godunov." The words were English and the voice was deep and friendly. Harold felt as if a weight was being lifted off his shoulders. He took a step back to get a better look at the officer and was impressed by what he saw. The uniform was spotless and freshly pressed. As a matter of fact, he had never seen a cleaner Russian uniform. There were three clips of decorative ribbons neatly and equally separated from each other pinned on the breast pockets. The Captain's face was cleanly shaven and his hair was almost white and closely cropped.

Harold didn't know what to say and waited for the officer to continue. The old veteran kept silent and motioned to Harold to continue to help himself and then escorted him to a small bench in front of an empty table. "I am Vadim Pajari and a friend of the Kommissar," he introduced himself in passable English. "You can stop your charade as a drunk anytime now. When you are done eating we will talk in my room." He looked as if he was slightly amused at Harold's appetite and his voice was even friendlier than before.

"I am supposed to meet up with Major Tesslov." Harold stuffed his face with the good tasting onions, "after his break," he added.

"Don't worry about the Major. He will find us when he is done sleeping," the Captain chuckled thinking about Tesslov. "You better get used to his frequent 'breaks'. There are not too many he passes up." Harold listened to the Captain not quite understanding the meaning of his words. He knew Major Tesslov now for over a week and he had never seen him just grabbing a girl like he had a few minutes ago.

The Captain noted the incomprehension on Harold's face. "You will learn. So far you have only seen the Major when he was near the Kommissar. Once you travel with him for a while you will understand."

Harold wiped the last bits of food from his lips.

"May I ask you a question, Captain Pajari?"

"Go ahead." The Captain was still smiling and his eyes rested friendly on Harold.

"What just happened? I mean the Major just grabbed a girl away from another officer and no one stopped him. I don't think that it was a rape. I have never seen anything like it."

The Captain got up before answering and gestured to Harold to follow him. "Oh, that was not unusual. Tesslov took advantage of a freebie."

"What?" Harold did not get it.

"Harold, that is your name right? Didn't the Major tell you

that this is a 'House of Joy'?"

"Nooo. What is a house of joy?" Harold felt a bit uncomfortable asking.

"How old are you?" the Captain asked. Godunov had told him that his protégé was a bright boy. If he believed it, he must have been too fast in his assessment.

"I am almost fifteen years old."

"That's what I thought the Kommissar said. He didn't mention that your comprehension is lacking."

Harold's English was not so great and he knew that the Captain's English was not perfect either. He wondered what he was missing. "Sorry, will you tell me?"

Captain Pajari shrugged his shoulders. "Why not? This building is used to offer entertainment for our soldiers. Most of the women here are Polish troop followers. There is no rape going on, but it is also frowned upon to bring your own. The lieutenant who caused the fracas at the door was an idiot."

Some of the answer went over Harold's head, but he got the gist of it.

"So, if I understand correctly, the troop followers are doing it for the fun of it?"

"Yes, at least more or less. I think." Pajari was not eager to follow up with more of an explanation. They had reached the room that had been assigned to him. Harold gathered there must be some kind of management or order in this facility because Captain Pajari assured him that Tesslov would find them.

"Do you know who occupied this place before it became a house of joy?" Harold asked as he sat down.

"No, but it would not take much to find out. Why do you want to know?" Captain Pajari went towards a cot in the corner of the room. He fumbled through a backpack and when he came back to the table he had a large bottle of Vodka in his hand.

Harold knew that his time was limited and he was worried that the Captain might fall asleep if he finished the bottle. He was also afraid that his questions might alert the Captain as to his true motive for asking.

"I know that in German times this castle served as headquarters for civilian officials. But, I know nothing about the particular unit of the Soviet forces who captured them." He hoped that his question was innocent enough.

Captain Pajari pushed the bottle aside as his eyes drilled almost into Harold's mind. "What took you so long?" His voice was still friendly and his eyes had not lost their sparkle.

"What....what do you mean?" stammered Harold.

"Don't worry. I did not mean to scare you. However, you should know that the Kommissar informed me of your parents and also that your mother died as a consequence of being in the wrong place at the wrong time." He noticed that Harold was concentrating hard, straining to understand every word.

"We kind of anticipated your inquiries. I for one am pleased that you did not disappoint us."

Harold thought for a moment about how to respond. "Thank you. I am glad that you understand. May I ask you, who is 'we' and 'us'?"

"Oh, I meant myself and the Kommissar."

"What about Major Tesslov?" Harold pressed the point.

"Yes, you could call Major Tesslov one of us. I guess." The Captain played with the unopened bottle and spun it on the table top several times.

Harold was not quite satisfied. "Am I one of us too?"

"You are pretty bright, Harold, but, you should learn to think before you open your mouth. Here is a question for you. We heard that Zampolit Kozlov got ambushed and killed. Did you have anything to do with it?"

"I heard about the unfortunate incident. I think that I was in Kommissar Godunov's office at the time it happened." Harold supported his answer with a blank expression on his face.

"Good, I like the way you said that. Now just in case that another incident would happen, let's say to a member of the unit who interrogated your mother, would you again be in a neutral, verifiable place?'

Harold started to understand where this was going, but at this point he still failed to comprehend the full scope of their discussion.

"Yes and no, Captain Pajari. I admit that I am bent on avenging my mother. However, I don't know where I will be when this happens."

The Captain had not taken his eyes off Harold and nodded a

silent consent. "Harold, just for a moment please bear with me because I have a vested interest in your answer. If you knew the identity of the unit or the responsible individuals, you would not hesitate to kill them?"

"Again, Captain Pajari, yes and no. The war is over and I don't intend to kill anyone. I will just make them wish they were dead." Harold's expression had changed and now it was Harold's blue eyes that drilled into the Captain's without a single blink.

"Slow down, Harold. Leave the inquiries to us. Concentrate on learning our language and customs. You need this now more than anything else." He opened the bottle and hesitated for a moment before he pushed the Vodka to Harold. "Care to try a sip?"

"No, thank you, Captain." Harold shuddered in disgust. He didn't want to disappoint the officer, however, he hoped that drinking Vodka was not on the list of requirements.

Nine

The door opened and Major Tesslov walked in. Without so much as a greeting or acknowledging the Captain's presence he reached for the bottle, took a long swig and looked for a cot to lie down. A second later he started to snore.

"Let him sleep it off." The Captain pulled Harold towards the door. "Come on; let me show you what this place is about."

They were on the third floor of the castle and Pajari explained that the rooms along the long hallway were bedrooms for the visiting officers. They went down to the second floor which was reserved for the actual activities and in front of each room stood a line of soldiers waiting their 'turn', as the Captain called it.

"Do you want to join them? Go ahead it is free." Pajari pointed to a short waiting line at the first of the rooms. Only four soldiers stood in front of it. When Harold didn't answer right away, the Captain took it the wrong way. He thought that Harold didn't want to wait.

"Step back, you animals. Let this boy go first." He pushed the waiting soldiers back and started to bang on the door.

"No, no," Harold stuttered in disgust. He freed himself from the Captain and took a few steps backward.

"What's the matter with you?" Pajari was not sure what to make of the boy but stopped when he saw the dread in Harold's face.

"I don't understand you German youngsters. No fear of fighting or dying, but when it comes to the fun part of being a soldier you chicken out." He kept on mumbling something in

PARTNERS TO A DEGREE

Russian and waved at Harold to follow him down the staircase.

It was now late in the evening and just as many soldiers were entering the building as were leaving. The Captain steered them towards some open rooms at the end of the great hall.

"How do you like this?" He pointed to a bicycle leaning against the wall. Right next to it were pieces of clothing, jewelry and all kind of ill-gotten gains. The soldiers milling around the room were busy trading whatever plunder they wanted to exchange.

At the entry to each of the rooms sat a junior officer who inspected each item the soldiers were carrying out. It seemed to Harold that he was issuing some kind of a certificate for the examined objects. The officer also entered a description of the articles in something like a notebook and collected a small tribute in return.

At first it made sense to him because it looked like an orderly procedure. That was until he noticed odd exceptions. Some of the soldiers made the clumsy attempt to conceal part of their booty and apparently got away with it.

"What are the rules that the officers let some of the items slide? I don't see them issuing a piece of paper or entering it in their books."

Pajari looked in the direction of the door guards. "But they always pay a fee?"

"I don't know. Let me pay closer attention." He observed another soldier leaving with a paper bag of goodies. "If I am not mistaken he paid a hefty fee for an uninspected item." Harold was pretty sure that he was correct.

"Well, I am glad that you noticed. It shows me that you are very observant." The Captain helped himself to a bottle of Vodka standing on one of the tables in the food area and turned back to the staircase. "We should get some sleep. Tomorrow we will drive to Warsaw."

"What about the items that are smuggled out?" Harold wanted to know.

"Nothing to worry about. They will get recovered. In the meantime it is one of the privileges of being an officer to collect fees from a stupid soldier." Pajari climbed up the stairs.

"Don't stand there with your mouth open. You will learn."

Back in the room they saw that the Major was still snoring away. There were several cots in the room and Harold selected the one furthest from the door. His mind was still filled with the warm memory of the day and of his father when he finally fell asleep.

It must have been the middle of the night when the door squeaked. Harold pushed the piece of the blanket, which covered his eyes, to the side. There was some light coming from the window and he was about to shout and wake the officers when he had to blink twice to make sure that he was seeing right. Nobody came to harm them. Instead it looked like a soldier was carrying a heavy but only medium-sized case into the room. It was more than strange because he had never heard of intruders bringing presents. The soldier didn't waste any time looking around and left as quietly as he had arrived.

Harold wanted to inspect the carton but decided to wait a few minutes just in case the soldier came back. It was a good decision. Nobody came back, but it looked as if the Captain had also been awakened. Harold saw him sliding from his bed and crawling over to the box. After several unsuccessful attempts to open the top the Captain gave up and returned to his cot. It was pretty obvious that he was disappointed because from time to time Harold could hear him cursing.

While he waited for the Captain to fall asleep he got drowsy and fell asleep himself.

"Time to get up." Major Tesslov was getting dressed and roused his roommates. The mystery case was standing where the visitor had left it. It was still closed.

"Where did this come from?" Harold acted astonished.

"Special delivery from the Kommissar. We will take it with us." Tesslov looked from Pajari to Harold. "I take it that you spent some time together. From now on we will only speak English and Russian to each other. If you don't understand what we are talking about you need to tell us. We will clarify using either language. But, no more German."

After a fast breakfast they took the box to the car that was still parked behind the hedge. Based upon their behavior it looked to Harold as if the officers were old friends. Tesslov was driving, following temporary Russian road signs to Berlin. It was not long before Harold realized that the Major had no idea where he was going. When they hit a familiar crossing for the third time he decided to speak up.

"We are essentially driving in circles. Any place you are looking for?" His English was still marginal and he had to repeat himself until the officers understood.

"I am searching for the fastest route leading east." Tesslov was studying a road map while looking at the mess of Russian, German and English road signs.

"Why didn't you ask me," mumbled Harold in German, but loud enough to be understood by Tesslov. "I said 'only English or Russian'. Now, where do I need to turn?"

Harold took over as a navigator until they ran out of German signs. Once they entered Poland they were at the mercy of the road map. However, most of the former highways had been pulverized by the tanks and there were no official thoroughfares.

It took them nearly two days until they reached Warsaw. Harold used the time to ask questions and while his Russian vocabulary increased, he had an awful time expressing himself coherently.

He also learned the meaning of the term 'time for a break'. The Captain did his best to educate him in the ways of the soldiers while Tesslov helped with pertinent curses and phrases.

Harold enjoyed the friendly and helpful efforts of the officers. Maybe they were due to his relationship with Godunov or the Russians were less disciplined. They were in stark contrast to the German officers who had sometimes treated him like dirt.

In Warsaw they were met by another political Kommissar. The Major knew him and addressed him without any formality by his first name. "Sergio, my old friend. I did not expect to see you this soon." He walked up to the Kommissar and embraced him but Harold noticed that it was not a heartfelt hug. The hugging seemed to be a regular Russian custom, similar to the hand shake in Germany, where no one hugged each other. Sergio had waited for the package. He was eager to inspect the contents and opened it without hesitation. Harold was surprised that it contained nothing but documents. He had expected jewelry or some other stolen goods and looked at Pajari for his reaction. At first it looked as if the Captain couldn't care less. He seemed more interested in looking out the window.

However, as soon as the new Kommissar was done sorting through the papers, Pajari offered to place them back in the box. There was no obvious reason to do so because they were now neatly arranged in small stacks on the table with the exception of three documents which Sergio had placed in his briefcase.

"Yeah, try to keep them separated and in their present order. I will send my driver to pick them up." Sergio nodded his consent and while he walked out of the door, Harold noted that Pajari had sticky fingers. Several papers stuck to them and found their way into the side pockets of the Captain's uniform. The Major had followed Sergio to his car and Harold was alone with Pajari.

"Let me help you," Harold offered, trying to catch a glimpse of the various letterheads. To his astonishment they were all in English and looked like British documents.

"That's nothing of interest. Only lists of food deliveries the Americans still owe us." The Captain was aware of Harold's interest and closed the carton before Harold could read any of it.

That's definitely not what it is, decided Harold. The documents were British and as far as he knew the British did not supply anyone with food or, for that matter, with anything else.

The next day they were ordered back to Berlin. This leg of the trip turned out to be more difficult than the first. There was total chaos on the highways and Harold could not help noticing that there were more troops standing still than were moving. It really looked to him as if none of the Belarusian regiments were going anywhere.

"What's going on? I thought that the war is over. Why are all your tanks rolling westward?" He could not help himself from asking.

"They are rolling westward?" repeated Pajari instead of answering the question.

"Yeah, as far as I can see they are either just standing around or moving towards the sunset," Harold insisted.

The Major who had followed the conversation said something unintelligible to Pajari and faced Harold.

"Why should this be strange?"

"I don't know if I would call it strange, but you asked me to be observant and to ask questions. We have been told that the fighting troops are going home. Supposedly to be replaced by occupation troops."

"And?" prompted the Major.

"I don't see any troops going east, except for the trains with the POWs."

"So, what is your conclusion?"

The Major knew now why Godunov had taken to the boy. He was no dummy. Perhaps a bit too young to understand the world of adults, but far brighter than most other boys his age. He wondered how Harold would answer.

"I don't have a conclusion because I don't know enough. But what I see is no different from what I saw when our army was getting ready for combat."

The Major looked again at the Captain before he answered.

"And you remember this?"

Harold shrugged his shoulders. "What else is there to remember? There was no circus coming to town."

Tesslov was taken aback. The boy was right and he had to answer in some kind of fashion.

"Maybe the military is planning on a maneuver with the western armies. I have no idea what the bigwig generals are planning."

Harold was not convinced. He had no strategic training, however, a maneuver this soon after the war and between agitated forces that did not speak the same language was highly unlikely.

"Right. Now, if you would tell me that your tank drivers don't know the difference between east and west I might believe it."

Harold was not intimidated. He had been subdued when the officers laughed at his naïve question about women and sex but this here was different. He knew the difference between withdrawal and offensive formations. If Tesslov and Pajari refused to tell him he would ask Godunov. Some of the things he had seen didn't add up.

Pajari enjoyed the gutsy answer and grinned from ear to ear. "I love our student. In a few years and with the right education he might be teaching us a thing or two."

"Well, Harold, we don't know the answer to your question," the Major lied. "Why don't we use the remainder of the trip to teach you how to drive?"

His divergence technique did not fool Harold who recognized the officer wanted to change the subject. It didn't matter. He kept on observing the slow but steady flow of armored cars rolling westward. But, more than that, he enjoyed the opportunity to get behind the wheel of the car. The driving lesson turned into a real challenge because the Major decided to give all his instructions in Russian which slowed the actual driving way down. By the time they were back in Germany and reached an improvised bridge leading over the Oder River, Harold had also learned a new set of words. Not all of them were automotive terms; however, they were all related to his driving efforts.

"Turn right at the next intersection." Tesslov was studying handwritten notes and an updated map he had received from their contact in Warsaw. "We should reach a small village and we will stay there overnight."

The main feature of the community was a rather old but extensive German field hospital. It was now being used by the Soviets and the entire facility sheltered seriously wounded soldiers. Harold observed that all the injured were Russians and Mongolians and he wondered what might have happened to the wounded German soldiers.

He also noticed that there were hardly any doctors around. The entire complex was seemingly being served by a group of German and Polish nurses.

"Park the car next to the church." Major Tesslov pointed down the street and left the car to enter the main facility.

"I better go with him. He might see a nurse and forget about us. It happens all the time." Pajari went right behind him and in a way he was right. He saw the Major addressing several nurses who had completed their shift and were on their way out. He was asking for the nearest field kitchen but was met with blank stares.

"Let me ask them." The Captain spoke Polish and repeated the question. He was immediately rewarded with an invitation to accompany the nurses to a mess hall down the street.

The officers beckoned Harold to join them and after a meal of soft boiled turnips and potatoes, Tesslov decided that he needed another 'break'. After several unsuccessful attempts to make himself irresistible to one of the younger girls he gave up and instead found comfort with a bottle of Vodka. Harold and Pajari left him sitting at the table and walked out in search of some kind of sleeping quarters.

"You should always follow these signs," the Captain enlightened Harold, pointing at a rude fence board featuring no letters but something like a symbol of a bed or cot.

"The whole occupation system is still in its infancy. We are used to sleeping when and where we can. However, now that the fighting is over we will need to establish some order."

After searching through several occupied houses they found one with folding cots in the hallway and two empty unfurnished rooms.

"This is odd," remarked Harold. "I have never seen an empty house without some kind of furnishings."

"Oh, I am sure that the houses in this village had furniture. They were part of the loot the Tatars are allowed to take."

"You mean to tell me that the Mongols emptied the houses?" Harold was stunned. He had seen the burned out German and Polish villages, but he had expected that the few unharmed and out of the way villages had been spared the ravages of war.

"No, not all of the homes. I think that they left the farm houses alone. But, if the home owners had more than just the bare necessities like chairs or beds they were subject to plunder. Don't forget that most of the common Tatar soldiers had never seen a cabinet or dresser." Pajari dragged a cot from the hallway into the room and motioned to Harold to follow his example.

"Should we get another one for the Major?" Harold looked at the hard bed without any coverings.

"No, he still might find a nurse to spend the night with. In any event, he will be at the car tomorrow morning. Sit down. I will get us some bedding from the hospital."

When he came back he had several clean blankets and even two pillows in his hands. "It's all there for the asking," he proclaimed.

Harold's head was still whirring from the driving lessons and all the new stuff he had learned. Sleep came fast, but not for long.

"Wake up, but be quiet. I need to listen." Pajari was rattling Harold's cot. He walked to the window and Harold could hear singing and yelling coming from further up the street. This was no cause to be awakened; the Russian's always seemed to sing at the drop of a hat. He looked at the Captain and the officer's demeanor gave him the feeling that something was not right. After a short minute of intense listening he stepped back from the window.

"Lock the door behind me. I'll be back in a little while." Before Harold was fully awake, Pajari was gone.

Ten

Harold stayed awake and tried to determine the reason for Pajari's concern. The singing had stopped but the racket continued for a long time. He cursed himself that he still was unable to comprehend full sentences. Some of the words he understood, however, the argument was heated and fast and he wondered if it was him or if he was listening to a different dialect or an entirely different language.

    A short time later, Pajari returned.

    "What happened? Are you alright?" Harold wanted to know.

    "I thought that I heard something of interest, but I was too late. The person I was looking for was not there anymore." The Captain lay down on his cot, preparing to pull the blankets over his head. "Go back to sleep. Maybe I'll find him in the morning."

    When Harold woke up he saw that the Captain was still sleeping. He got up to find a place to wash himself and went into the food hall, hoping to find a German-speaking nurse. As luck would have it, his very first questions were answered by two German women who were preparing food for the hospital patients. At first they were surprised to see a German-speaking boy in a Russian uniform but they turned out to be very helpful. They gave him a key to a fairly clean bathroom with running hot water, a luxury he had missed for weeks. On his way back he stopped to check on their car and saw the Major coming his way. He looked well-rested and a big grin covered his face when Harold asked him if he had experienced a peaceful night.

    "Harold, my boy, never worry about me when there are nurses around to help me through the night. I feel great. Where is the Captain?" Apparently he had slept through the ruckus because he didn't mention it.

While they were talking, Pajari showed up and engaged the Major in a rapid exchange. The Major was immediately interested in whatever the Captain told him but didn't show the slightest concern. However, after he had heard the end of the report he told Harold to reserve them a seat in the mess hall. While Harold returned the washroom key to the cooks, he observed the two officers heading in the direction of last night's disturbance. The ever-present hot tea was just right and he poured himself a second cup, dipping some freshly baked bread in it when Tesslov showed up again. Behind him was a Russian sergeant followed by the Captain. Harold thought that the group would join him and was surprised to see that they completely ignored him and took a seat on a bench by the window.

Well, if not then not, he told himself and walked over to the steaming soup tureen, which was filled with a watery looking barley soup. *Barley in the morning.* He didn't even like it in the middle of the day, but there was nothing else available and supposedly it was nourishing. He took his time eating. The taste wasn't too bad, maybe a little too spicy but otherwise good enough to consider a second helping when he saw that Pajari was making eye contact with him, indicating that he should follow him outside. As he stepped into the early morning sunshine he collided with the Captain who was already on his way back.

"Look hard at the soldier sitting next to us and burn him into your memory," he hissed in English and helped Harold up, cursing him very loud in Russian for his clumsiness.

Harold understood and after walking some steps in the direction of their car, he turned around and went back to his unfinished breakfast. From where he was sitting he had a very good view of the Russian, except that he had no idea how to burn him into his memory and wished that he had Karl's observation qualities. His friend had always been good at seeing and memorizing details. Maybe there was a way he could train himself in this art.

He noted that the sergeant's face was smooth without a single wrinkle, featuring a slightly oversized nose. He guessed his age to be late twenties and found himself focusing on his unusual short neck. It almost looked like the sergeant's head grew straight out of his wide shoulders.

Harold recalled that a teacher had told him once that the best way to remember something is by association so he searched his memory for a fitting similarity. Besides the dirty, dark, nearly black hair, he saw no other outstanding details.

The group had finished their breakfast and on their way out Harold caught a brief glimpse of the soldier's abnormal, almost colorless eyes. It was as if he looked into a bucket of water. Plain colorless water. At the same time a familiar picture flashed in his mind. A German newsweekly had featured a character named *'Wasserkopp'* (water head) in their cartoon section. It was a guy without a neck who had been born stupid, didn't learn anything as he grew up and stayed a dummy all through his life.

"Did you get a good look at him?" Pajari reentered the mess hall and sat next to Harold.

"No problem. Whenever you want to talk about him just say *Wasserkopp* and he will pop back into my mind." Harold was satisfied to have found a simple way to improve his memory. "Who is he and why do I need to remember him?"

"Later," answered the Captain. "The Major told me he wants to stay here for a while longer. I think he is experiencing a challenge with one of the Polish caregivers and we might not leave before tomorrow. We have plenty of time and this will give us the opportunity to extend your driving lessons. We also need to talk about a few things."

The weather had changed and was not exceptionally helpful. It had clouded up and a heavy rain very quickly turned the unpaved roads into a mess. Harold was a little disappointed. He had barely figured out how to maneuver through the deeper puddles, dousing 'by accident' some innocent bystanders when the Captain called their exercise good enough.

"I still don't know how to down-shift or how to turn the wheels so that I avoid drenching the poor soldiers," he protested loudly, but to no avail.

"Not today and not in the rain." Captain Pajari was sure that Harold knew exactly what he was doing and he had to stop him before he soaked the wrong officer.

"You wanted to tell me about Wasserkopp," Harold

reminded Pajari, sipping hot tea through a piece of rock sugar. The rain had increased to a downpour and they had settled in the food hall. It was far more comfortable than their bare room.

"As I said before, later. Right now it would be a good time to talk about you and your future." The Captain had searched for and found a few cucumbers, which he sliced into small spears and shared with Harold.

"Kommissar Godunov has assigned me to teach you a few basics before he sends you to the "Frunze" Academy in Moscow," Pajari began.

"I was under the impression that Major Tesslov was supposed to teach me. Do I now have two teachers and what is the Frunze Academy?" Harold remembered that the Captain had helped himself to some of the British documents. He was not too sure that all of the three officers, Godunov, Tesslov and Pajari had the same interests at heart. His own loyalty was foremost with Godunov and he decided to keep an open mind regarding the other two.

"Major Tesslov is responsible for teaching you sufficient Russian so that you are able to function on your own. The Frunze Academy is Russia's oldest military school. Kommissar Godunov intends to sponsor you, which in itself is a great honor, besides giving you the opportunity to begin a professional military career. However, the final choice is up to you. I am given to understand that you prefer a career in the intelligence branch." Pajari was chewing the juicy cucumber.

"Thank you," said Harold, "What are the basics you will be teaching me?" He was less polished and more direct than Karl would have been.

The Captain settled back in his chair. "I am a specialist in a very little known training program." He smiled to himself. "Little known, but, extremely effective. We call it 'Imagination and Goal Concentration' or IGC." He saw Harold's blank look and added, "I know, it does not translate very well into English. No need for concern. You will understand in due time."

"Sounds interesting. How does it relate to me? You said that you are a specialist in this program. Are you a professor and did you teach it at the academy?" Harold's ears had perked up the moment he had heard the term *extremely effective*.

PARTNERS TO A DEGREE

"I am an accredited instructor. I teach each year for a period of eight weeks at the academy, but enough about me. Your future will depend on how well you pay attention."

"I am ready." Harold had stopped eating. In order not to miss anything, he was mentally translating every English word and phrase into German. He wished that Godunov was teaching him.

"You told me that one of your present goals is to avenge your mother." He looked intently at Harold. "Suppose for a moment that this goal is accomplished. What's next on your agenda?"

Harold was not prepared for this question. He figured that somehow, someplace, things would fall into place.

Pajari could clearly see the befuddlement in Harold's eyes.

"You don't know? Alright, I'll help you." He pushed Harold's tea cup to the other side of the table.

"Close your eyes and listen up. Imagine yourself as a thirty-year-old submarine commander. Right now you give the command to dive. The sea is closing above the boat and you are settling on a southern course, 120 feet below the surface. Picture it. Now. Got it?"

"Yes, not clearly, but yes. I've got it," Harold answered.

"Good, keep your eyes closed."

Harold complied, not knowing what to make of the exercise.

"The first action to obtain what you want out of life is to decide on it. Period." The Captain paused for a moment to let it sink in.

"I know that it sounds simple, however, most people never realize that they need to decide, unconditionally, on a goal. They hesitate to decide because they want all kind of assurances. They almost always want some kind of guarantees which delay and most often stall their decision process."

Pajari spoke slowly. He wanted to convey the importance of his words to Harold.

"Picturing yourself successfully obtaining your goal will help with your decision. If you like what you see in your imagination then your goal warrants further examination. If not, then not."

Harold had still his eyes closed and listened to the Captain. It seemed that the voice he was hearing did not belong to Pajari. It was more like a mental path leading him into the future.

"Change your mental vision. Picture yourself as a thirty-year-old tank commander leading your regiment into battle with shells exploding all around you."

Pajari's voice was the same as before but now Harold imagined himself in a tank in front of the zoo bunker in Berlin. Buildings falling down and flames all around him. He didn't want to act against the Captain's instructions but he did not like what he was imagining. Not one bit. The picture in his mind seemed real even though he was fully aware that it was just his imagination.

"Change your mental vision again. You are a pilot, but not in the air force. You are a civilian and in command of a four-engine passenger plane, approaching Paris. You see the Eifel tower in the distance and you are ready to land the plane."

While Harold was somehow in a trance, Pajari gave him a minute before he told him to open his eyes.

"Which one of the pictures did you like the best?" he asked.

Harold shook his head. "Did you hypnotize me?" He had to think to find the correct English words.

"No, not at all. You seem to have a vivid imagination and with some training you are able to hypnotize yourself. But, this is not the object of this exercise. Tell me, which picture, I mean which mental picture did you like the best?" He smiled at Harold who was still a bit confused.

"No question. Flying to Paris was the best."

"Thank you, Harold. Or better yet, thank yourself. You know now what you don't want. This is just as important as knowing what you do want. In any event, the Frunze Academy can wait."

"Are you saying that I need to imagine every occupation in the world to arrive at the one I really like?" Harold didn't get the gist of the exercise.

"No, Harold. No need to even think that way. Plus, you are thinking too far ahead. Don't push yourself. However, you should know that your imagination is the greatest gift from your Creator. If you use it correctly it will always provide you with constant, unlimited energy to pursue any goal you decide on."

"I know that we humans have imaginations. It is supposed to be one of things which separates us from the animal kingdom, but I never heard that it generates energy. How does this work?" Harold was struggling with the double task of understanding English and comprehending the meaning of the lesson.

"Easy, Harold. You are pushing again. In time you will learn that your imagination will always provide you with power. Your imagination works in two ways. It either provides you with the dynamism towards your desired goal, or, if you picture an unwanted or scary picture, it will provide you with the tools to get away from it."

Pajari stopped again. He knew that he was heaping a load on the young boy. Experience had taught him that even officers at the Frunze Academy struggled to comprehend the full implication of the lesson.

"For right now, all you need to do is to listen. After a few days you will arrive at your own conclusions." He looked for a brief moment at the wet and streaked window panes.

"I am listening. What do you mean when you say that I am pushing it? I thought that I asked a simple question," Harold persisted.

"I could probably answer your simple question with a simple answer. If I chose to do that you will not really *experience* the mighty power of your imagination. You will only *know* about it."

"Maybe it's my poor English because I still don't understand. I thought you wanted to teach me and I was supposed to learn," Harold pressed.

"Right, I will teach you. Knowing that you have your very own imagination is not the same thing as using it. Just as knowing that you have a pair of eyes is not the same as using them. You have to open your eyes and use them to fully experience their magic."

The Captain wrote short instructions on a piece of paper.

"For your first lesson I want you to temporarily decide on a goal and when you go to rest tonight I want you to imagine yourself having reached that goal. That's all."

Harold looked at the paper. The Captain had written three words: "Use your imagination."

"Any goal will do?" Harold wanted to be certain.

"It would suffice to teach you the concept. However, let's make it more purposeful. You want to be an intelligence officer so picture yourself twenty years older, having reached your objective. Tomorrow we will discuss this further." There was nothing left in his cup so he got up in search of another pot of tea

As Harold watched Pajari walk in the direction of the kitchen, he had the feeling he was approaching a brand new level of understanding. The trip to Warsaw had been boring in comparison to his present anticipation. He experienced a momentary flash of joy as if there was nothing but unlimited opportunities around him. Maybe his imagination was already at work. He didn't know and was thankful that the Captain was his guide.

He must have been daydreaming and was startled when Tesslov stood suddenly in front of him.

"I need the keys to the car. Is there still any gas in the tank?"

Harold fumbled in his pocket and came up with the funny pointed car key. It almost looked like one of the wind up keys he had seen at his parent's house for an old grandfather clock.

"For all I know it could be nearly empty. Where do I get the gas?" He couldn't remember looking at the gas gauge.

"Walk through the village and look for trucks with gas drums. When you spot one come back and tell us. I doubt that anyone will share their gas with you so we will need to go with you."

Tesslov kept the car key and started to talk to Pajari, who had returned with a pot of boiling water. He reached in his side pocket and unfolded an old newspaper. There were some crumbs of black Chinese tea mixed with lint and what looked like pipe tobacco.

Harold looked on in bewilderment as the Captain carefully scraped it together and then dumped the mix in the steaming water. "This will have to do until the kitchen staff comes back," he announced as he sat down.

Tesslov was apparently used to this kind of brew because he stoically watched the debris swirling in the pot.

"Did you tell Harold about our guest this morning?" he inquired of Pajari.

The Captain shook his head. "No, I waited for you to return."

Tesslov thought for a second. "Hmm, we might as well tell him. So far no one else has shown up." He turned to Harold. "The sergeant who sat on our table, this morning? You remember him, the one without a neck?"

Harold remembered the Wasserkopp, he nodded. "Yes."

"Now don't get all flustered. His name is Egon Borovsky. He belonged to the detail that raped your mother."

Harold was stunned. "How do you know? Are you sure? Is he still around?"

"Oh yes. He bragged about it and identified the date as well as the Genshagen Castle in enough details. There is no question in our minds that he is one of the fellows you are looking for. His unit must be close by because he is waiting for his comrades to join him here."

Harold became agitated and didn't know what to think. Sure, he wanted to avenge his mother but he had never thought about how he would do it. And now, his two officer friends were just sitting there, seemingly unperturbed, slurping the terrible brew and watching his reaction.

He wanted to get up, not really knowing what to do.

"Sit down, Harold." The Major's voice was stern but friendly. "We had to tell you, but we don't want you to do anything. Not yet. We need this guy to point the way to the other culprits."

Harold squirmed around, but the look in the Major's eyes pinned him to his seat.

Eleven

"What will we do if morning comes and the remainder of his unit has not arrived?" Harold was anxious to know.

"There are other ways to identify his friends but don't worry, they will show up. He is strutting all over the village announcing the arrival of the heroes," the Major assured him.

"Are you saying that he is openly advertising another orgy?" the Captain asked.

"No, not really, but my nurse darling told me that he offered her 'compensation' if she could find some willing participants for his victory party."

"I wonder how many and what kind of 'victory parties' these guys are planning," speculated Pajari. "He identified his unit as the 'Champion of the Castle'. At least that was what he said last night when I heard it the first time. If he would have kept his mouth shut I would have never noticed him."

"Did he tell you how many soldiers or officers are in his outfit?" Harold had simmered down, hoping to discover additional details.

"He was talking about twenty or twenty-five soldiers with a captain being in charge. However, he mentioned that the interrogation of the female prisoners was the doing of a special squad. Four sergeants, including himself."

"Besides labeling his team is there any official record of his squad?"

"Yes, Harold. We, as well as Kommissar Godunov, knew right from the beginning the identity of the company itself. But due to the ongoing exchange of the fighting regiments with the reserves, we temporarily lost the exact whereabouts of individual teams."

Harold was astonished that his two officers were apparently gathering data on his behalf.

"I want you to know how much the information means to me."

This was the best he could do to express himself. Secretly he wondered if Tesslov or Pajari would help him if push came to shove.

The Captain seemed to read his mind. "If you are serious about becoming an intelligence professional you will need to learn that correct and timely information will be your greatest asset. So, use it wisely and build upon it. In due time you might even wish to act on it, but not now."

Harold understood that he would be on his own if he acted too hastily. He knew that the officers were right. He needed to know the identity of the whole squad. But, just in case they didn't show up, he tossed around several scenarios. None of them amounted to a plan A or a plan B.

"If it is alright, I will go and look for a fuel truck." Harold got up and left the room.

"What do you think, Vadim? Will the boy restrain himself?" Tesslov asked his friend.

Pajari replaced their obnoxious potion with fresh tea from the kitchen before he answered. "Hard to predict. We haven't known him long enough. However, I know what I would do."

"Yeah, I know. This is also the reason why you are still a captain and I doubt that you will ever get another promotion," Tesslov provoked him.

"You should talk." Pajari could have answered with a more suitable comment but he let it rest.

"So, are we continuing to Berlin tomorrow or do you plan on another day of rest?"

He thought about the British documents in his pocket which he needed to get into the hands of General Berzarin, Berlin's city commander, as soon as possible. He didn't know what kind of information they contained, but Godunov's orders had been explicit. He was to intercept the transfer of the documents in

Warsaw, look for some specific papers and deliver them personally to the general. At first he had been puzzled by the order, wondering why Godunov didn't hand the documents to Berzarin himself, until he realized that the Kommissar was already on the way to the funeral in Moscow when the courier left Berlin. Or was it Potsdam? Come to think of it, he really didn't know the origin of the transport.

"If we are able to obtain the necessary gas tonight we will leave in the morning. In any event, I would like to be in the city by the evening," answered Tesslov.

*****

Harold had a difficult task ahead of him. There weren't many trucks parked alongside the road and the only vehicles in the side streets were horse-drawn farm wagons. He didn't see a single fuel drum on any of them. He speculated that there could be a fuel depot in the nearest town. Frankfurt on the Oder River was only a few miles away.

"Have you heard about the party tonight?" a female voice interrupted his thoughts as he passed the nurse's quarters. He recognized the northern accent. It belonged to the German woman who had allowed him to use the wash room in the morning.

"Yeah, I heard about it. But, you might not wish to participate." He thought of warning the cook somehow.

"Oh, don't worry, I never attend any of the Russian celebrations. Too much drinking going on. I just thought you would be interested. It should be fun. Some of our younger Polish nurses are looking forward to it."

"Where is the party supposed to be?" He trusted his officers, but figured it wouldn't hurt to do his own investigation. To get the individual names of the culprits was one thing, to scorch their actual physical identity in his mind was another.

"So are you going?" the cook asked instead of answering.

Harold was surprised by the slight intensity in her voice and didn't know what to make of it. It could not possibly be that she was interested in him. He had no experience with girls because he had never dated one. Admittedly, the woman was not bad looking, but at least five years his senior. "No, I don't think so. I don't drink and don't know how to dance. Why do you ask?"

"I hoped that you could help us."

"Help you? How? By going to the party? And, who is 'us'?"

He was getting better at asking questions. Karl had been a good teacher.

"Come with me to the kitchen and I will make you a sandwich with pig lard."

The idea of getting a bite of his favorite sandwich would have been sufficient for Harold to follow her anywhere. He could not believe his good luck.

"My name is Harold. What's yours?" He watched as she heaped a princely amount of the precious lard grease on a slice of bread. He knew it couldn't get any better than that.

"You can call me Hilde," she answered as she handed him the delicacy. "I will give you the remainder of the tin, if you help us."

"Alright, what is it that you want from me?" The blubber was oozing from the bread and he licked his lips.

"I want you to meet two wounded soldiers. We have been hiding them from the Russians."

"Are they Wehrmacht (German Army) or SS?" Harold was not willing to help any member of the Storm Troopers.

"They are regular foot soldiers. They need better care than we can provide."

Harold had his mouth full and had to swallow before he asked: "What does this have to do with the party tonight?"

"We would like to take them to a different place and we saw you driving a car today. The party should draw any lingering Russians from the street."

"Who is 'we'? And, how far do we need to drive?" He was almost done with the sandwich.

"Gertie, the other German cook, and me." Hilde prepared another slice of bread. "Not very far, maybe two miles at the most," she added, handing him the second treat.

Harold was thinking as fast as he was chewing. "I'm not sure that I will be able to get the car. Do you know where the Russians gas up their cars?"

"I think there is a gas depot further down the road than we need to go." Hilde looked hopefully at Harold, who wiped his hands on a rag.

"I'll let you know," he went to the door. "Give me about an

hour."

He could still taste the lard on his lips when he bumped into a soldier passing by. "Pardon me," he said in Russian and looked into the blank eyes of Egon, the Wasserkopp.

The sergeant mumbled something and went on his way. Harold, however, was stunned. He was so close to his target and yet he didn't know how to proceed. For a second he considered going back to Hilde and sharing his situation with her but he could not imagine how she could possibly help him. Before he could make up his mind to follow the sergeant or not, he saw a truck loaded with newcomers stopping in front of the main facility.

The noise coming from the new arrivals indicated that they were slightly intoxicated. It also looked as if some of the soldiers had recognized Egon, who had also stopped to squint at the group. A moment later they exchanged greetings and the sergeant lead all of them to a house across the street. His friends had arrived.

*****

"There is no fuel truck in sight but I found out about a depot a few miles from here. It also seems that Egon's comrades have arrived," he announced to the Major, entering their housing.

"Oh, then we will see who is attending the event." Tesslov smiled in anticipation. Harold wasn't sure if he was referring to the soldiers or the nurses. It looked as if the Major had already started getting warmed up as there was a half-empty bottle of Vodka on the table. No glasses, but it seemed that Tesslov was more inclined to attend the festivities than to go for a ride to obtain some fuel.

"Why don't you observe how our student drives in the dark, Vadim?" Tesslov asked his friend. "If I see more than I can handle I will save you one."

"Thank you for not starting without me. You are being too kind." The Captain took the car keys from Tesslov. "Let's go." He motioned to Harold to lead the way.

"I don't know exactly where the depot is; I only heard about it from the German cook. I will ask her to show it to us." Without waiting for an answer Harold let the Captain get the car while he went to see Hilde.

"You need to show us the fuel station," he declared. "I want to see where you want me to drive your soldier friends," he added when he saw the hesitation in Hilde's face.

The car was equipped with the regular seat benches. Hilde sat next to the door while the Captain was driving. Harold had jumped into the center and this enabled him to communicate with Hilde without speaking.

She pressed his hand and tilted her head as they passed a place where three small houses huddled together. It was very close to the fuel supply and the Captain allowed Harold to drive on the way back. In addition to filling the tank they had also loaded up with several five-gallon metal cans which Harold stored behind the last seat bench. He paid careful attention to the dark road and to Pajari's surprise he avoided most of the puddles. But he was not fooled by the boy's good behavior. It was possible that Harold wanted to impress the pretty cook, but then he suspected that Harold's suspiciously good driving was due more to the total absence of soldiers.

Over an hour had passed since Egon's unit had arrived and the singing coming from the building indicated that the party had started. "Why don't you go in and save me a seat? I'll join you after I park the car." Harold stopped in front of the brightly lit entrance.

Pajari looked first at Harold and then at the young cook. A wide smile crossed his face. Maybe his boy was growing up. He got out but then turned around. "Take your time, but return before the Major misses you." He winked knowingly at the girl and walked through the door without looking back.

"What was that?" Hilde wanted to know.

"I don't know," answered Harold. "Maybe he thinks that I wanted to kiss you." He was a little ashamed to even think about it.

"No, that's not it." Hilde had just turned twenty and was certain that kissing was not all that was on the Captain's mind.

"Hurry up and get Gertie to help us carry the wounded to the car." Harold didn't waste any time wondering about the Captain's comment. He had pulled up the car to the nurse's quarters and wanted to get on with the transfer. The earlier, the better. He knew that within a short time the drunks would spill out onto the street.

Hilde led the way through the nurse's quarters to an outbuilding. It looked like an old chicken coop except that the chickens were gone. They had been killed before the war had ended. Only the dirty smell still lingered on.

It was dark in the room. Hilde's dynamo flashlight allowed Harold to see a bunch of straw bales alongside one of the walls. They provided an excellent hiding place. There was no trace of the soldiers until Hilde removed one of the lower bales.

Harold had to crawl in order to follow her. He had expected something like another room behind the hay, but all he saw was a hollowed-out niche in which two soldiers were resting. Hilde was already tending to the first one. One of his legs had been amputated and he was obviously in a very bad shape and heavily sedated. Gertie pushed a makeshift stretcher towards them and Harold tried his best to carefully roll the wounded on top of the blanket between the two pieces of wood. In spite of the dark, they had the soldier out and into the car in no time at all. The women were more experienced than Harold and knew exactly what to do.

He wanted to get back to retrieve the second soldier when he saw to his surprise that the fellow was right behind him. He had one arm in a sling and on the other side there was just an empty sleeve stuck to the shoulder. He flashed a thankful smile to the girls and curled up on the floor of the car next to his comrade. Gertie stayed behind and Harold put the car in gear. Again, he was carefully avoiding the potholes; this time for a more compassionate reason.

Their timing could not have been any better. The party was in full swing and the road was deserted. Harold had figured that the complete transfer would take close to an hour but to his relief it was much faster.

Hilde pointed him in the direction of the exact building and as soon as he stopped the car they were surrounded by several women who carried the amputee away. Within a few minutes they were on their way back. It happened so fast that Harold never knew the identity of the soldiers. He was satisfied that he had been able to help and his eyes followed Hilde when she jumped out of the car.

"Wait a moment," she called, running into her quarters. When she came back she handed him the small tin with pigs lard. It was almost full.

Before he could say *thank you* she hopped on the running board and kissed him. It was so different from the kisses he was used to receiving from his mother that Harold was speechless. It seemed that her mouth had lingered a second longer than was necessary to make contact with his lips and in that short moment it had triggered a strange, but wonderful sensation. By the time he had recovered, Hilde was gone.

Unsure what to think he parked the car, took the tin with the lard to his room, and went to find his officers. Pajari noted Harold's flushed face and poked him in the ribs. "You could have stayed a while longer. Dummy."

"Wh ...what do you mean?" stammered Harold, still not in command of his feelings.

The Captain shrugged his shoulders. "Nothing. However, if you don't take your time...you will never learn." He used his thumb to point to the Major who was scribbling in a notebook.

"We have the names and the identities of Egon's squad." He turned his head and nodded at a table close to them. "They are over there."

Harold recognized the Wasserkopp and glanced nonchalantly at the soldiers sitting next to him. "Are you sure?" he asked the Major.

"Oh yes, we are sure. They talk about nothing else except bragging about their activities." Tesslov turned his eyes to the Polish nurses sitting next to the sergeants. "If these girls could understand the Russian language, they would not be drinking with them."

Harold could hardly understand the Major. The noise in the room was deafening and the occasional shouts between the chanting were nearly earsplitting. He saw a loaf of the dark Russian bread on the table.

"May I take this to our room?" he asked, hoping to make himself another sandwich before the bread was gone.

"Go ahead and take some of this stuff along" Pajari lifted a few bottles from the neighboring table. The owners of the Vodka were busy dancing in the center of the room and Harold wondered briefly if this would lead to a confrontation later on. The Captain filled Harold's arms and gently pushed him out the door.

"I doubt that I can manage." Harold objected to the load, but found himself alone in the street. He tried to get a better hold on the bottles but the bread started to slip and landed in front of his feet.

He decided in favor of the bread and left two of the bottles in the shadow of a fence post. He could always pick them up later. Making the sandwich was easy compared to sorting out the thoughts which filled his mind. There was the Wasserkopp with the dreadful eyes. He should now be on his target list because the officers knew the identities of the other perpetrators.

There was also the task of remembering their features and, to his irritation, he could not shake the memory of Hilde's kiss from his mind. Matter of fact, he hoped to catch a glimpse of her on his way back to the party.

First things first. I need to remember their faces. He spread some lard on a slice of bread and placed it on a chair next to his bed, hoping it would be soaked all the way through by the time he came back.

The next ten minutes found him unprepared.

Twelve

Harold was almost in front of the entrance when the door opened and a drunken soldier stumbled onto the street. For a moment he stood there, not singing, not bawling, a twinkling cigarette dangling from his lips. He was frantically trying to find his balance and to stand upright. Then he crashed headlong on his face.

Well, it's started, Harold thought and walked a step faster to get to his officers. When he passed the drunk he noticed the wide shoulders and the absence of a regular neck. Next thing he knew, his reflexes kicked in and he was kneeling next to the body, lifting up the head. No mistake. It was Wasserkopp.

Harold's mind swirled. Here was his chance, but he didn't know what to do with it. It would have been easy to grip a rock and smash in Sergio's head but as much as Harold's basic values had changed in the past weeks, he was not ready to kill.

In a flash of anxiety, his mind told him that he had waited for this moment and that he had to do something. He quickly looked around and found he was alone with the sergeant. Nobody was coming or going. He pulled the unconscious body a bit deeper into the shadows, away from entrance. Now what?

His heart started to beat in an increasing staccato and Harold felt like it was going to burst out of his chest. His mind was churning with possible scenarios but above it all, it was as if he heard Pajari's advice. *Use your imagination* he had said.

Harold's mother appeared in his mind, begging Egon for mercy.

In an instant Harold made up his mind. He raced to the two

Vodka bottles he had left behind. Somebody had told him that a solid tap on the side of the head would not kill, but severely jiggle the brain. He lifted the first bottle and smashed it against the sergeant's temple. In his excitement he must have aimed too low because a part of the bottle hit the hard ground and broke into shards. The booze flooded over Egon's face and over the upper part of his uniform. In his mind, his mother was still there, pleading for her life.

Without thinking and as if in a trance, he took the second bottle of Vodka and drained it over the sergeant' lower body. He drenched the pants and then pressed the empty bottle under the body. The cigarette was still glimmering a few feet away.

He picked it up and blew some life into it. Sparks were flying and on the second try the alcohol caught fire. Flames flickered around Egon's pants and then advanced upward to his face. It was hardly a fire, but it was progressive never the less. An unknown impulse triggered within him and Harold started to scream at the top of his lungs. It seemed that all his suppressed emotions were combined in his screech. The door opened and soldiers spilled onto the street. Harold gave the impression of swatting at the flames and when the soldiers threw clothing on the twitching body, he stole away from his victim.

No one noticed his disappearance. The soldiers were drunk and too busy dousing the flames. They succeeded and in spite of the bad burns, the sergeant was alive.

"What was the shouting about?" The Captain wanted to know when Harold sat down at the table.

"I have no idea," lied Harold. "I was with Hilde for a moment."

Pajari looked at him. The boy was obviously agitated. His face was flushed and his hands were trembling.

"That's my boy, Harold is finally growing up." The Captain turned to Tesslov to share the excitement. However, the Major seemed to be badly in need of another break as his attention was firmly centered on a pretty Polish nurse.

"Watch the Major, Harold. He is setting an example. Come on and share a drink with me. You have a reason to celebrate." He pushed a bottle of booze in Harold's direction.

Harold's tension had eased and in all reality he almost felt like celebrating, however, for a different reason. He accepted the first drink of his life and twenty minutes later he was spilling his guts all over the place. His thinking was impaired and he was sick to his stomach as never before. The Captain had to carry him to their room.

When morning dawned, Harold found himself in miserable shape. The Vodka had done a number on him and he had a difficult time waking up. It was his first hangover and he vowed never to drink again.

"It seems that we don't have to worry about our friend Egon anymore," Tesslov announced as he entered the room. He had spent the night with the cute nurse and seemed to be in an excellent mood. He was ready to pack up and get going.

"Egon? What happened?" Pajari wanted to know.

"Apparently he had an accident and set himself on fire."

"Is he dead?" Harold's stomach was still in convulsions but he was interested enough to ask.

"No, I understand that he will live, but I doubt very much that he will enjoy it." The major discovered the greasy bread on Harold's chair. Without asking he took a hearty bite. He was sure that Harold would not object and he was right. Harold could not even bring himself to look at the tin of lard. However, he got up and forced himself to chew on some dry bread.

"What happened?" Pajari wanted to know.

"Well, from what I heard, Egon will never see again. The flames must have gotten to his eyes." He finished the pigs lard sandwich.

"I also understand that they might have to amputate his ding-a-ling. In any event, he will never molest a woman again. It was a very unfortunate accident." The Major was done with his report. He was still smiling and wiped his face on a piece of towel.

"Indeed," commented the Captain and looked intently at Harold who made believe that he was still puking his guts out. Despite his meager comprehension of the Russian language he had understood the gist of the conversation.

"I'll drive today and you can sleep it off," the Major decided while he watched Harold carrying their few belongings to the car. The boy was clearly sick.

"I'd like to visit the hospital, just to make sure." The Captain left the room without specifying what he meant.

*****

"How is the burn victim?" he wanted to know when he arrived at the main building.

"He will survive, but he lost his eyesight," confirmed one of the elderly nurses, "and, maybe more," she added.

"I need to talk to him, where is he?" Pajari walked towards the room which was reserved for the critically wounded.

"You can see him, but you will not be able to talk to him until a few days from now." The nurse tried to be helpful to the Captain and Pajari stopped and turned to her. "Is there anyone who saw what happened?"

"The soldiers who carried him in last night didn't tell us. We know that his injuries were caused by burning alcohol."

"That's all?" Pajari continued asking.

"Yes, except that he also suffered a concussion. He must have hit his head when he passed out."

"And, then he proceeded to set himself ablaze? How did that happen?"

"We assume that he was smoking and carried an open bottle of booze in his hand."

"Is this in your official report? May I see it?"

"We will file one when we are done. The sergeant is still facing a serious surgery. Please come back tomorrow." She looked at Pajari's solemn expression and felt that she had to say something to comfort him. "I feel very sorry for your friend, Captain. It was an unfortunate accident."

Pajari nodded his head in agreement. "Yes, it must have been. This is the second time that I heard this sentiment."

The nurse was called away and left Pajari standing in the hallway. He walked out the back way and entered the kitchen. He wanted to have a word with Hilde, but her duty didn't start until late afternoon. He couldn't think of anything else to do and went back to the car.

The Major was coming from the nurse's quarters and Harold had used the opportunity to make a quick trip to the mess room. He was sitting, grimacing and bent over, behind the driver's seat.

"What do you think about this accident?" Pajari asked his friend once they were on the road. He purposely used a dialect unknown to Harold.

"What do I think? Our boy is very capable. I am proud of him," the Major answered. His smile had not left his face since the morning.

"I agree. He did this without training and left no trace. He is better than I ever was." Pajari tried to remember the exact timeframe of last night.

"No, he is not better; there is none better than you. But maybe..." Tesslov searched for the correct term and found it. "Maybe he is more resourceful."

Pajari remembered something. "Hey, Harold, wake up. Where did you put the bottles I gave you last night?"

Harold was drowsy as he turned around and retrieved a full bottle of Vodka. "Here is one. I hope you don't make me drink again. The other one is here too." His short trip to the mess room had been successful.

"Dang, I would have sworn there were no bottles in our car. This made me wonder because I remembered that Egon was not carrying any booze when he staggered out of the room." In his excitement he slipped and spoke regular Russian.

Tesslov broke into loud laughter. "What did I just tell you?"

The Captain said nothing. He was glad that the boy was not his enemy. He also noted that Harold had understood the last part of the conversation.

*****

When they reached Berlin, they split up. Harold stayed with the Major and Pajari went to see General Berzarin to deliver the documents.

The city commander was surprised when he saw the English letterheads and then he seemed disturbed when he tried to decipher the writing. He told the Captain to wait in the guard room. As soon as Pajari left his office the general called his own translator.

His first guess proved to be correct. The documents referred to a 'secret' meeting of the western allied field commanders on the 16th of June. Some place in Berlin. He presumed that the meeting was secret because no one else had told him about it and he was the officer in charge of Berlin.

June 16th was only a few days away and he decided to visit

with Marshal Zhukov to determine if he knew anything about it.

But first he sent a runner to fetch Captain Pajari.

"Who told you to bring these papers to me?"

"Kommissar Godunov, Comrade Berzarin."

"Godunov gave you these papers?"

"No, Comrade Berzarin. The Kommissar told me to intercept a document transfer to a Kommissar in Warsaw. I was supposed to look for these documents and then to hand deliver them directly to you."

"When was that?"

"Two days ago, Comrade."

Pajari didn't tell the city commander that there was a whole shipment of additional documents. For all he knew they could have been a decoy and never intended to make it to Moscow. He had hated this assignment from the beginning and cursed himself for not knowing what was going on.

"Two days ago," exclaimed the general. "What took you so long?"

"I ran out of gas and had to stay down for a day. Major Tesslov was with me and can attest to it." Pajari did not like the general's outburst and tried to offset it by mentioning the Major. He should have known better.

"That figures. Were there any women where you ran out of gas?"

The general was only forty-one years old but highly decorated and experienced. He knew that Tesslov worked directly for Godunov but he also knew about the Major's escapades. He tried to figure out why the Captain was traveling with the Major and why the Kommissar had sent the Captain to deliver the papers instead of sending Tesslov. He took another stab at it.

"Does the Major know that you intercepted the messenger?"

"No, Comrade General. The Major knows nothing about it".

Now it got really confusing, but general Berzarin was nobody's fool. He was determined to get to the bottom of it.

"Do you have another pressing assignment or can you stay with me until tomorrow?"

"I am able to stay with you until the Kommissar returns from Moscow. The funeral of the Zampolit is today. I should be able to serve you at least until the day after tomorrow."

PARTNERS TO A DEGREE

He was not directly worried about himself, however, something was not right and he felt it in every bone of his body. Silently he wished that he could be with the Kommissar. In any event, at this point in time he felt safer with the city commander than with the Major.

"Good enough," answered Berzarin. "I want you to come with me when I see Marshal Zhukov."

"Now, Comrade General?"

"Either tonight or tomorrow morning; I'll let you know. You will be assigned quarters in this building,"

The city commander dismissed the captain and sent a message to Marshal Zhukov requesting a meeting.

*****

Only a few days had passed since Harold had said *goodbye* to Karl but in that short time, a few things were changing the landscape of Berlin.

All of the Allied forces started to stake out their territory, or sectors, as they called it. The Soviets occupied about half of the city and more or less kept to themselves. The Western forces established a British and an American sector. All of them agreed on some crossings, which were called check-points.

On the first evening, after their arrival from Warsaw, Harold was able to slip through a subway tunnel to his friends in the Berliner Strasse which was now in the British sector. Frau Becker was happy to see him well and healthy and promised to keep his written message for Karl. It consisted of only seven words:

"Karl. One down, three to go. Harold."

He dated it and placed it in a blue envelope. He had not seen a white envelope in months. It didn't matter and he figured the blue envelopes must have been some kind of a left over from military surplus.

Herr and Frau Becker wanted him to stay for the night, but Harold refused. He had promised the Major that he would be back within three hours. He made it in less than two.

The short trip had cost him his Russian coat and pants. The stench and filth from the subway water had ruined them. Hopefully the Major would be able to secure a backup uniform.

He needn't have worried. The first one to greet him upon his return from the Becker's was Alex. The Tatar was about to embrace him when he sniffed and backed up. Harold didn't blame him, the stink was a bit much. Alex grunted a few times, took the filthy rags from Harold and left the room. It didn't take long and he returned with a nice ensemble. Not only was it clean but it was also much better fitting than his previous outfit. He grinned his Mongolian smile when he handed it to Harold.

The underwear was not a problem. Harold had a second set in his satchel.

"How did he secure the uniform?" Harold had noted that Alex had given the Major some kind of a report.

"Leave it to Alex," Tesslov smiled too. "He had cornered a soldier and simply asked him, in his unmistakable sign language, how long it would take him to exchange his outfit before he needed his personal assistance. Apparently this was all it took."

Karl had asked Harold to *'take good care of the friendly giant.'* If Alex's behavior was any indication, it was the other way around. The Tatar did not move from his side and Harold figured that he had inherited him.

"Where is Poti and how did Alex know how to find us in this awful place?"

Harold didn't like the place at all. It was located in the Moabit section of Berlin. His father had once described it as the most rundown area of the city. He didn't know if it was true, however, the old tenement building in which they were staying gave him the creeps. There was no running water and no bathroom. The toilet was in the hallway of the building and in 'normal' times it would be shared by four tenants.

"This meeting place had been arranged by Kommissar Godunov, before he left for Moscow. Poti was already here and will be back by tomorrow," the Major explained.

Why had Godunov decided on such a decrepit place? Maybe it was due to the fact that it was one of the few buildings which had survived the war without a scratch. He had noticed a few unharmed buildings in the immediate neighborhood and he had no idea if this was by sheer luck or if the Soviets had spared the housing of the common laborers on purpose.

The Major noted Harold's discomfort. "I see that you don't appreciate this flat but I am sure that you stayed in worse places."

Harold looked at the high, bare brick walls, no wallpaper

and only a few splashes of paint here and there. He flinched. "No, not really, unless you consider the subway tunnels. This whole area stinks of people without ambition. It is a slum. I have never seen anything like it. Even our makeshift accommodations in the flak towers were definitively superior."

He looked up at the unpainted ceiling and shuddered again.

Thirteen

Major Tesslov seemed to be amused by Harold's comments and reaction. "Well, Harold, I hate to tell you, but you will encounter far worse accommodations in your lifetime."

"This might be true but if you were to break my back and legs, I would still find a way to crawl away." Harold wanted to add what he thought of people who lived voluntarily in places like this, but stopped himself in time. No reason to elaborate. Tesslov apparently had orders to stay here.

"How long will it be until the Kommissar returns?"

"He should be back within the next two days." The Major made himself comfortable on a field cot. There were about five of them folded up in a corner. Harold opened one up for himself and then helped Alex to do the same. The Tatar indicated that he would not mind sleeping on the floor but flashed a thankful smile at Harold when he was done.

"Is there any way that you could help me understand Alex? Maybe you could teach me just some basics?" Harold asked, thinking that it would be nice if he could communicate with Alex.

"Yes, we should make the most of our time together. It will not be a waste of effort because it will help you in your career. However, I think that Godunov will dismiss Alex pretty soon."

The next two days were filled with language lessons and when Godunov arrived he enjoyed listening to Harold's efforts at communicating with him and the Major, first in the Russian language and then in Buryat.

Tesslov had been wrong in predicting that Alex would leave

them. However, he was right that the Kommissar had no further personal use for the Tatar. Godunov seemingly liked the mutual efforts of Alex and Harold trying to understand each other and he ordered the former to stay with Harold at all times.

Shortly after Godunov's arrival, Pajari returned from his previous assignment with the city commander. It seemed odd to Harold that he immediately requested a closed door meeting with the Kommissar.

It only lasted a few minutes.

"Harold, I want you to make contact with your civilian friends in the west sector. Poti will drive you. He has the necessary papers to pass through the check points." Godunov took Harold aside, out of earshot of the others.

"What do you want me to do?" Harold was eager for some physical action instead of studying.

"I know that there are still some SS Werewolf units in the city. I want you to find out if they have a hideout in the neighborhood of 'Neukoelln'. (City district of Berlin) However, I don't need to know their exact locations. " The Kommissar handed Harold a pack of tobacco and about half a pound of black Russian tea. "This is all I have to offer to your friends".

"I don't think that I will need to bribe them. They don't like the SS any more than I do." Harold didn't think he would need the support of Alex on this trip, but the Tatar insisted on going along.

*****

"This makes no sense!" exclaimed Marshal Zhukov when he met with General Berzarin. "There is no meeting planned. But I will call our western counterparts, just in case we missed something."

The city commander was not fully satisfied. In his opinion the Marshal did not examine the documents thoroughly enough. Zhukov didn't even bother to call for his own translator. It was apparent that he was not interested in extending any effort into finding out what the papers were about. Berzarin didn't get them back either.

A day later he was notified by Marshal Zhukov that there was no planned meeting and that he should mind his own business and stick to his job as a city commander. The notice had been short and rude and Berzarin wondered if it was really a personal note from the Marshal.

He conferred once more with Captain Pajari and then sent him back to attend to Kommissar Godunov's need. He decided to find out for himself.

The next morning, on the 16th of June, he called for his guards to assemble a small motor unit, including some motorbikes, and took off to inspect the suspicious meeting point.

A few hours later he was dead.

Immediately after the announcement of his death, rumors started to fly around the city and the allied headquarters. The Soviets declared that he had been assassinated by an SS Werewolf unit. They had received a tip from an unnamed Russian political officer and combed the basements in the surrounding area of the accident. Surprisingly, their search turned up a few SS men who refused to surrender, and no one decried their deaths.

The western army intelligence conjectured that if it was an assassination, then it was the work of the Soviet Secret Service. They had the whereabouts in place and despite missing an apparent motive, had somehow lured the Russian city commander into an ambush. The Americans flat out rejected the idea of the Werewolf unit because no weapons or explosives had been involved.

The German's thought that it was a simple automobile accident. After all, the Russian drivers were not too skilled and caused many accidents. The civilians mourned the demise of the Russian city commander. He had been a compassionate officer who had established order and shelter for the homeless and his generous field kitchen had fed the starving population.

*****

"Well done..." Harold heard Godunov saying to Pajari and missed the remainder of the sentence because the Kommissar had switched into a dialect he did not understand. It could have been anything Godunov was referring to and Harold had his own idea when he saw the true bewilderment in the Major's face when the news broke. Whatever it was, he was sure that the Major was not a part of it.

Late in the evening, Harold was questioned by the Kommissar as to his whereabouts when Egon, the Wasserkopp, had set himself on fire. Godunov had heard about the incident from the major.

"I don't know when the accident happened. To the best of

PARTNERS TO A DEGREE

my memory I was either with Hilde, the German cook, or with the officers," Harold lied, looking straight into the gun metal grey eyes of Godunov. "The Captain got me drunk," he offered as an excuse of not correctly remembering.

"Good enough, Harold. Just don't forget, lies are harder to remember than the truth."

Harold shrugged his shoulders. How could he ever forget the Wasserkopp?

"What did Hilde say to you? I mean when you parted." Godunov fired the question, baffling Harold. He had absolutely no idea what he would have been possibly doing with Hilde much less than what Hilde would have said when they were done. However, he still remembered her kiss.

"I wish Karl was here. He would take me out of the hot seat." He looked kind of embarrassed at Godunov, hoping to divert him. He seemed to succeed

"Yes, Karl would have helped you out. By now he should be happy and reunited with his family." Godunov got up to leave the room and turned around before he reached the door. "But Karl could not have done what you don't remember you did."

Harold was glad that the Kommissar did not press the point. For a moment he felt the need to tell Godunov that he had observed the Captain swiping a few documents in Warsaw but then he remembered that he talked too much.

When he suppressed his urge to share what he had witnessed, it also occurred to him that it was time to observe and retain. The present guessing game about the true cause of General Berzarin's death was the perfect reminder. He observed that there were just too many and different theories floating around and that he didn't know enough about any of them.

He was only sure of two things. The head of the Soviet Union was Joseph Stalin and he was known to eliminate anyone who stood in his way. He did it all the time and in an open and direct way. However, Berzarin's unfortunate accident had not been open and direct. It stood to reason that it was not Stalin who had given the order or had anything to do with the General's sudden death.

But someone wanted him out of the way and succeeded.

Harold found himself guessing. *Observe, retain and keep your mouth shut*, he told himself over and over again.

Based upon his previous discussion with the Major, Harold had been under the impression that they would stay a few days with the Kommissar in Berlin. He was surprised when Godunov sent him on a different mission in the morning. He was to accompany Major Tesslov to a high security prison camp in Luxembourg. At first he was not sure why he was traveling with the Major because they had to drive deep into American occupied territory, even crossing a part of western Germany.

He was even more confused when Alex was also ordered to go along. He surmised that the Tatar was really a bodyguard for the Major. But he was wrong.

"You know of course what is in the boxes," Tesslov pointed to the cardboard cartons next to Alex in the back seat.

They had crossed into Luxembourg and stopped short of their destination. The Major had been quiet during their trip while Harold had continued his effort to communicate with Alex. He was making pretty good progress. Godunov had been right when he thought that Harold had an affinity for languages.

"No, I have no idea. I don't even know why I am here," Harold answered honestly.

"Well, they contain the propaganda reels you discovered for the Kommissar in Berlin. We are to deliver them to the American commander of the prison."

Harold had to think back. He remembered Godunov's eagerness to get his hands on the German propaganda films identifying places as well as the names and positions of the leading Nazis. This was during the first days when Karl and Harold had been doing favors for the Russian Kommissar.

"You are here to attest as to how and where you found them," continued the Major.

He didn't wait for an answer because he didn't want to elaborate on the subject. A short time later he stopped in front of the old and prestigious hotel Mondorf-les-Bains. The high electrified fence attested to the fact that it now served as an interrogation center.

If the Major had thought that he could just wave his credentials to get into the building he was sadly mistaken. The American guards took his ID's and his orders and then made him wait. Finally, a US major allowed them access to the facility. Alex was forced to wait in a separate guard room and it took all of Tesslov's skill to make Alex understand that Harold was not in any physical danger. The Tatar was pacing back and forth in the small room, cautiously eyeing an American sergeant who kept his hand on his sidearm.

The American officer in charge of the prison was a colonel with the name of B. Andrus. He politely listened to the Russian major and spent more time interrogating Harold about the source of the documentation than looking at the actual reels. Tesslov was glad that Harold was able to back up his explanations with correct references as to the source and the timeframe of the recovery.

It turned out that the American officer was very familiar with the unsuccessful attempts of the Allied forces to obtain the Nazi propaganda films in the first place. They had searched for them to provide the Allies with supporting documentation during the upcoming Nuremberg trials. It was due to Godunov's quest and Harold's knowledge of the subterranean entrance to the archives of the German propaganda facility that the Soviets were now in a position to deliver the valuable documentation to the Americans.

The whole visit lasted a little longer than two hours because the Colonel dictated a receipt and a letter of gratitude to his aid. He wanted to be sure that he maintained the proper protocol with the Soviets. The receipt was addressed to Marshal Zhukov and the personal letter of gratitude was addressed to Kommissar Godunov.

When the Major and Harold returned to the guard room to claim Alex it looked to all concerned that he had finally given up. He sat somberly on a chair in a corner. His head was down and something was definitely wrong with his equilibrium. When he got up to join Tesslov, he stumbled from one side to the other and finally fell down in front of an American sergeant. It was the same soldier who had drawn a gun on him in an invitation to sit down.

The sergeant felt sorry for the obviously disoriented Mongol and extended a hand to help him up. Harold wanted to shout something in Buryat but could not think of the correct term. It would have been too late anyhow because the hulk stumbled again and this time he came crashing down on his right elbow. Due to his massive weight he would have surely shattered his joint if he had not landed on the center toes of the left foot of the unlucky sergeant. After the soldier's screaming subsided, it was determined that the toes were broken. The sergeant would limp for a long time.

Alex humbly excused himself as he staggered toward their car. The American watch commando stared transfixed at their groaning comrade on the floor. All of them agreed that it was a very unfortunate accident. One of them remarked that it was a case of one in a million that the Tatar's elbow had been saved by the toes of the sergeant. Instead of leveling a charge against Alex they wished the departing major goodbye and helped their friend to the first aid station.

"What?" grunted Alex when Tesslov reprimanded him, "I could have hurt myself."

"Right," answered Tesslov, "and pigs can fly." It was a remark he had picked up from the Americans and neither Alex nor Harold knew what it meant. It did not translate very well.

In his final report to Kommissar Godunov, the Major briefly mentioned the incident in Luxembourg and Alex's unsteadiness. Godunov was neither amused nor surprised. "Everyone who knows Alex also knows that he stumbles. A lot. It is not his fault. Must have something to do with his inner ear," he concluded, smiling.

In the meantime Harold went out of his way to search for something special for Alex to eat. When he didn't find anything he 'borrowed' a few onions from the Major's private reserve and shared them equally with his friend.

"I have given some thought about your relationship with Alex," Godunov addressed Harold the next morning.

"He can travel with you as long as you are on assignments for me. During this time the army will provide him with food and care. However, once you decide on an academy or learning institution you will need to assume all responsibilities for him. I will provide you with some funds during this time. Not much, but you will get by. You need to understand that should you decide to keep Alex with you, your financial resources will be severely limited."

The Kommissar had spoken in Russian and Harold wanted to be sure that he understood correctly. "Are you saying that you can decide on Alex's future, or give him away like a pet? I thought that Alex would be released from the army and sent home."

Godunov nodded his head. "Sure, the Tatars did their job and are being dismissed from the military. They are free to go wherever they wish to go. However, Alex is different. He was a full orphan when he joined the forces and he has no friends and no place to go. If you don't wish to support him I will assign him as a prison guard to some camp in the Ural Mountains. Not much of a future but I guess it would be better than being homeless."

Harold did not have to think twice. "I will keep Alex with me and when I enter an academy I will find a way to support us." He was pretty sure of his abilities and the academy was light years away from today.

"Not to worry, Harold. I only wanted to test your resolve. I needed to hear from you some kind of commitment. When the time comes I will provide for Alex's needs." He turned to leave when Harold asked him to stay for a moment.

"What's on your mind, Harold?"

"Not much. I would just like to know if the war is really over. None of our troops are going back to Russia. It really looks to me that there are more and more units coming in from the east and they all mill around between Warsaw and Berlin."

"Hmm, it seems that you are gifted with an extraordinary talent of observation. Now if you would pair this with keeping questions to yourself, you will go a long way in our intelligence services."

Harold thought that he was already practicing keeping his mouth shut. "Karl said the same. Nevertheless, he always asked questions to keep learning."

"Asking a question to learn something is reasonable. Asking a question when the answer is staring you in the face is downright stupid. And," the officer continued, "I don't think that you are stupid." His voice was almost gentle.

"We should turn this around. From now on I want you to observe whatever seems to be out of the ordinary. And then, when we meet, I don't want you to ask me any questions. Instead, I want you to give me your conclusions. This will make you think for yourself and prove to me that I have been right about you."

"Alright," said Harold. "In this case it is my conclusion that the Soviet Forces are poised to continue this war. Maybe all the way through France and to the Atlantic coast."

The Kommissar shook his head. "You are arriving at a huge conclusion without any supporting data. You only observed the tanks and the troops standing still and 'milling' around. So what? Have you seen any ammunition or food accumulations? Have you observed any fuel or medical supplies being shifted westward?"

"No," admitted Harold, "I have not thought about it."

"Wrong answer, Harold." Godunov's voice became a bit harder.

"Wrong answer?" repeated Harold. "It is the truth. I have not thought about it."

"No, that is not what I mean. If you would have said that you arrived at your conclusion too early and that you were willing to spend more time observing, I would have accepted it. But simply saying that you have 'not thought about it' is not good enough. As a matter of fact, it implies certain laziness on your part. I don't ever want to hear you say something like that again."

He left the room without giving Harold another chance to reply.

Fourteen

Harold had to admit that the Kommissar had a point and he realized that there was a hidden lesson in the scolding. It was not so much that his mind was lazy and that he wanted instant answers. No, it was more along the lines that he recalled several independent actions of his officer friends which had raised unanswered questions in his mind.

He had observed that the relationship between the Kommissar and the Major was different from the relationship between the Kommissar and the Captain. In spite what Pajari had told him, there were definitely different agendas involved.

He also realized that the Major had gone out of his way to make it possible for him to see his father. He knew that Tesslov had acted on his own without any input from Godunov. Why? He came up with two possible answers. Either Tesslov had an interest in assuring himself of Harold's support further down the line, or, Tesslov was a genuinely nice guy.

Then there was the theft of certain documents by Pajari and he was wondering who was acting upon whose orders. He also recalled that Godunov had originally wanted the propaganda reels for himself, which was the opposite of handing them over to the Americans.

And, what about the sudden demise of General Berzarin? He could not believe that it was a simple accident. He was sure that someone would ultimately reap benefits from his death.

All in all, he decided, he needed more information. Matter of fact, a lot more, if he wanted to put the bits and pieces together he currently had. And that was exactly what consumed him the most because he remembered that one of the officers had told him that accurate and timely information was the greatest asset of an intelligence officer. He was no intelligence officer, not yet, but just the idea of it was interesting and tempting.

He had plenty of time to gather the missing pieces. In the meantime, he decided, he would increase his observation and cut down on his questions.

*****

The next day Harold was ordered by Godunov to drive with the Major once more into Poland. There had been some unrest between the Polish civilians and Jewish refugees. The command to prevent hostilities and to instill order had come directly from Marshal Zhukov. This was a difficult task because the local Polish authorities refused to cooperate with any and all instructions from Russian officers.

Major Tesslov's orders were to observe and to identify hot spots. Harold was again behind the wheel and he enjoyed the double chore of learning the Russian language and driving. He also appreciated that Godunov had ordered one of his personal bodyguards, Yefim, to come along with Alex.

Their first destination was the medium-sized town of Ostrava in the previous provincial district of Galicia in southern Poland. The further they drove to the south, the closer they also came to the Czech - Slovakian border.

"Fuel transports," Harold remarked, when after a day of driving they reached the outskirts of Ostrava. A seemingly endless column of fuel trucks rolled from Slovakia towards the west. Harold had to stop, unable to make a left-hand turn into a cross street leading into the city. The fuel convoy was not moving very fast but didn't slow down either when Harold resorted to his horn to call attention to his predicament.

None of the Russian drivers paid any attention, however, the sound had awakened Alex who looked at the situation and then motioned to Harold to simply cut off one of the trucks.

"They drive too close behind each other," Harold answered looking helplessly at the Major beside him. Tesslov agreed. Any turn would cause a collision.

Alex looked around for foot soldiers but there was only the

long snake of trucks coming in their direction. He took off his uniform jacket and folded it neatly on his seat and then walked a few steps up the road. Reaching into his pants pocket he retrieved a pack of cigarettes and jumped on the running board of the next truck. Waving the cigarettes in front of the windshield he used his other hand to grab the driver's long hair and almost pulled his head out of the cab. Unable to see anything, the driver stepped on the brakes and stopped the truck.

Alex waved at Harold to use the break in the formation to make his turn and then offered the driver a few cigarettes in return for a match. The Russian driver who had feared losing his hair stared at the giant and could hardly comply fast enough. Alex smiled at him, tapped him gently on the shoulder and jumped off the foothold. A moment later he was back in his seat with his jacket across his lap.

"Why didn't you use the power of your political star emblem?" Harold asked.

"We only identify ourselves when there is no other option; besides there were too many of them," answered the Major.

"Alex didn't think so." Harold could not help himself.

"Agreed, your friend does not think." The Major reached into his own pocket and offered Alex a packet of cigarettes as replacement.

When Harold noted an abundance of very good looking Polish women in Ostrava he knew that the Major would be tempted to take a two or three day 'break'. Tesslov did not disappoint him. As soon as he had secured quarters for his detail, the Major excused himself until the next morning.

There were some old buildings in the center of the town that had somehow survived the fighting and Harold used the free time to admire the ornate décor. If it would not have been for Alex and Yefim it might have been a bit of a risk to walk in the Russian uniform through the town. The Polish civilian population had no use for the Soviets and made no attempt to hide it. They did, however, have enough sense not to bother the two Tatars.

*****

"Good morning, get up, we are leaving." Tesslov showed up much earlier than Harold had anticipated.

"Are we driving home, already?"

"Our mission here is over. I found out what the Kommissar wanted to know. But we will make a detour to Krakow just to confirm a few things."

The trip to Krakow was an eye opener for Harold.

"What do you know about the German extermination camps?" The Major was barely in the car when he started the conversation.

"What is an extermination camp?" asked Harold in return.

"So you don't know that the SS maintained concentration camps and killed systematically hundreds of thousands of inmates?"

"I heard about concentration camps, but not of mass murder."

Tesslov considered for a moment Harold's answer. It might be that the boy spoke the truth. Most of the camps had been outside of Germany and the few which were inside the country had not been near or in the vicinity of Berlin.

"Tell me what you know," he prompted again.

"I know that the SS arrested anyone who said anything derogatory about Hitler. They also rounded up the mentally ill and any unproductive people."

"What do you know about what happened to these people?" Tesslov persisted.

"We were told that they were forced to work in ammunition factories."

"And you, or your friends, never wondered why none of the prisoners ever came back?" The Major probed.

"No, not really. The war was raging on several fronts and demanded a constant stream of ammunition and war material." Harold answered without hesitation and Tesslov believed him.

"Alright, Harold, relax. This is not an interrogation. I only wanted to know where to start."

Harold had a difficult time believing what Tesslov told him during the remainder of the drive. While he had witnessed the brutality of the SS, he was shocked to hear about a Nazi concept that the Major summarized as ethnic prosecution.

"Now the talk about war criminals and the upcoming trial in Nuremberg is making sense to me." He was finally able to respond. However, he could not bring himself to believe everything the Major told him.

Tesslov understood the doubt he saw in Harold's eyes. "I see that you don't wish to accept what I told you, and you don't have too. The Nuremberg trial will provide the evidence and proof."

Harold reflected on their trip to Luxembourg and on the extraordinary questions from the American officer. In his mind things were falling into place.

"Which way to the Kleparski Square?" Tesslov inquired when they reached the center of Krakow. His command of the Polish language was not too good but still astonished Harold. There seemed to be no end to the abilities of the language wizard.

Within a short time they reached the Kupa Synagogue next to the square. It was a Saturday. Harold pulled up close to the entrance and while they waited for the Jewish service to end, he observed a group of Polish boys gathering stones and broken pieces of bricks.

"That's how it usually starts." The Major had noticed it too. He got out of the car and ordered some lingering Russian soldiers to disperse the kids. It didn't do much good. The Polish teenagers simply vanished into the side streets and when the soldiers left they showed up again in greater numbers. And, with more rocks.

Tesslov disappeared for a moment behind the carved wooden doors of the synagogue and returned with two Jewish worshippers. As he pointed to the waiting teens he advised the two peasants to stop the congregation from leaving until he had some soldiers in place to assure their safety.

"How can I help?" asked Harold, not knowing what to expect.

"Drive forward and block the entrance, but don't get out of the car. Alex and his friend Yefim will stay with you while I get a Polish administrator." He gestured across the town square to some official looking white enamel signs on the largest building.

Harold eyed the neighborhood for some support from Russian soldiers but for one reason or another, the plaza was empty. Except that some civilian adults had now also gathered around the boys and it seemed that they were encouraging each other.

"Move over." Alex pressed Harold against the door and sat next to him, protecting his side from any possible stones flying towards the car. They didn't need to worry. Tesslov was already on his way back with two Polish civil servants in tow. None of the two spoke a word of Russian but were fairly fluent in German and Tesslov's German was much better than his Polish.

"How do you intend to protect the worshipers?" Tesslov wanted to know, gesturing towards the growing bunch of onlookers.

"This is none of our concern," the taller one of the two bureaucrats answered. The other one nodded in agreement. "They should have stayed where they belonged. Preferably hidden."

"You are in charge of maintaining order," the Major thundered.

"We will have order when the unwanted are back in Galicia or wherever they were hiding from the Germans," the shorter one maintained, cowering from the glaring eyes of Tesslov.

"You care to explain?" The Major was unyielding.

"I'd be only too happy to do so," the taller and older one obliged. "Before the war we had about 60,000 of their kind in our city. They confined themselves to a small area in the Kazimierz section of the town. When the Germans came and hunted them down, their numbers dwindled to about 2,000. Now, just a few weeks after your troops supposedly freed us, we are again faced with over 6,000 and we don't want them."

"What do you mean, you don't want them? They are Polish citizens just like you are."

"No, they are not, and as God as my witness they will never be. But, we don't harm them like the Germans did. We are only looking the other way when our young people make it clear that they are not welcome."

Both of the Polish supervisors grinned at each other, enjoying that the crowd around them was growing and Harold feared that it might turn into an angry mob. Some of the spectators understood German and supported their elders with shouts of encouragement.

"If you don't establish order within the next few minutes you will regret it for the rest of your very short life." The Major's eyes conveyed confidence when he turned the lapel from his jacket around, exposing the star of the dreaded GPU.

The smiles on the faces of the civil servants froze. Nobody in the Soviet occupied territory would dare to challenge the Communist Secret Police.

"How....how do you want us to do this?" The taller one was clearly terrified. His eyes darted from the Major to the Tatars and back.

"Now that's your problem, isn't it? You will tell your people to disperse and not to come back. If I see any teenager lingering around, I will take you and your stupid looking assistant for a ride. You might as well say *good bye* to your friends because you will not return."

At the same time the Major exposed his star Yefim had leveled his side arm at the taller man's head and gestured to the frightened bureaucrat to move closer to the car. There was no question that the Major meant business. The threat to be taken away in a vehicle of a political officer was more than the man could handle.

He yelled at the top of his lungs to the civilians, urging them to leave the plaza. At first there was no movement, except from some of the older ones who started to shuffle away.

Alex had followed the proceedings without moving from Harold's side until the Major identified himself. In the very next moment he was out of the car and grabbed the other civil servant before he could run away. True to form he twisted an ear of the hapless man causing him to shriek in pain. The screaming and pleading of the official caused the remainder of the bystanders to disburse.

"I want you to gather food, water and blankets and bring it to the Synagogue," Tesslov ordered, and the two supervisors complied as fast as they could. With the help of several store keepers they delivered a heap of supplies during the next two hours.

"What else do you wish us to do?" The merchants as well as the civil servants stood sweating in front of the Major.

"Who is the most respected citizen in your town?"

"That would be omrade Grodzki."

"Good, bring him here." The Major waved at the merchant who had answered and motioned to the other ones to remain. Within the next hour Tesslov sent for additional senior citizens and by the evening he convened a meeting in the town hall and installed a new city government with Grodzki being the new city administrator.

"Should I hear any complaints from the Jewish community I will come down on you like a load of bricks," he assured the assembly. "Keep your youngsters under control." After this last warning he took the new administrative team over to the Synagogue to introduce them to the Jewish worshippers.

"I hope that your problems are solved. Keep the supplies as a reserve," Tesslov informed the congregation and advised them to stay overnight in the building. He was convinced that he had not resolved the underlying issues but for the present time he had restored some order. He trusted that Grodzki would be more up to the task than the former official.

"The Jewish faith needs a homeland and even then I doubt that this will solve their difficulties. The distrust between the ethnic groups goes back a very long time and I am sure the incidents we observed in Krakow will erupt over and over again," Tesslov told Harold during the drive to the next small town. The Major had no desire to spend the night in the city.

Harold drove all the way to Oppeln (later named Opole), a town in Ober Schlesien (Silesion). By the time they arrived it was very late. For a second time the streets were congested with fuel transports and Harold noted that they were all in route to a certain section along the Oder River. When morning broke he saw endless rows of parked Lorries. It looked very much like an organized depot.

*****

Back in Berlin, Tesslov reported immediately to Marshal Zhukov and Harold had an opportunity to visit with Godunov for a short while. At first he wanted to update the Kommissar with his observations but then decided to wait until he had more to report.

"Did you see anything worth mentioning?" Godunov was in a very good mood. He had heard from his daughter and he was thankful that she was recovering without any serious side effects.

"No, except that the Polish population does not appear to be very happy with our occupation."

"This is no news. Anything else?"

"No." Harold remembered the previous reprimand and was not ready to volunteer half-baked opinions.

"Well, you should have noticed something, but I see that you are learning." The Kommissar was busy sorting through the paperwork on his desk. "I like your progress with the language lessons, however, I need the Major to stay with Zhukov. Hopefully you will do equally well with Captain Pajari."

He had found what he was looking for and stuffed some of the papers in his briefcase. "For the next few months you will be traveling with the Captain. I expect you to absorb everything he teaches you. And, I mean more than just the languages. He is a very smart man."

"One more thing, Harold." Godunov rounded his desk and stood in front of the boy. "When is your birthday?"

The question caught Harold off guard and he tried to figure out today's date. Ever since he had been traveling with the officers it had been a whirlwind of activities, one day blurring into the next.

"I must have turned 15 a few days ago," he answered, surprised that he had forgotten his own birthday.

"That's right. I am thinking that instead of a present I will offer you a piece of advice." His grey eyes made contact with Harold's.

"To whom in this world do you owe your greatest loyalty?"

Harold struggled with the answer, not knowing how to respond. "I don't know about loyalty. I am devoted to my father...,"

He could see the disappointment in Godunov's eyes and took it the wrong way. "And I am devoted to you and Karl," he added.

"I feared that you would say something along those lines. But, devotions aside, you only owe loyalty to yourself." Godunov's voice was serious, but friendly.

Harold was not convinced that the statement was true. He thought of it as rather egoistical. Never-the-less, it was good advice because it told him something about the Kommissar's mindset.

"Thank you, Herr Godunov. I will not forget it."

Fifteen

Two days later, Harold was with Captain Pajari and Alex on the way to the seaport city of Stettin. Shortly before, he had been called into Godunov's office.

"Are you up for a delicate task?" The Kommissar was holding an envelope in his hand.

Harold nodded, not knowing what to expect.

"Captain Pajari's mission is to bring a pouch of documents from the city commander of Stettin to Marshal Zhukov in Potsdam. I want you to add this envelope to the papers without the Captain's knowledge."

"What will happen if I am unable to do it? Is there anything specific you want me to do with this letter?" Harold was confident that he could intercept the pouch. On the other hand he had to know if he needed a backup plan.

"No, just destroy the letter. I will know within a day if you did not succeed."

Godunov did not seem too worried and Harold wondered if the 'delicate task' was a scheme to test his ability. Or, maybe to test Pajari's proficiency. He did not underestimate the Captain and looked forward to matching skills with him.

"Consider it done," he assured the Kommissar and looked at the writing on the envelope before he folded it and stuck it in his pocket. It had only two words printed on the outside: *Marshal Zhukov.*

They followed a road on the east side of the Oder River towards the Baltic Sea and two hours out of Berlin they were rerouted. Harold could see a massive gathering of T34 tanks on both sides of the road. Because of the many repair teams working on the vehicles, he speculated that they were being readied for further employment.

"Where do you think the tank crews are?" He had to keep his eyes on the car in front of him to stay with the detour.

"I can see a fair amount of dark grey tents further up along river," Pajari responded. "They are too far away to ascertain if they are sheltering troops or supplies."

"Hmm, what kind of supplies would need the protection of tents?" Harold probed.

"Don't know. I am pondering the same question." The Captain raised a pair of binoculars to his eyes and scanned the area surrounding the tents.

"Well, this is most certainly curious and warrants taking a better look. Turn left on the next crossroad. This might be something of interest to the Kommissar." He reached inside his coat, assuring himself that his GPU emblem was within reach. Alex sensed the tension in the Captain's voice and pinned his own ID on his chest pocket.

"Stoy!" A military motorcycle cop crossed in front of them, holding up his hand. He had seen the car's departure from the main road.

"Turn around!" The MP was serious.

So was the Captain. "We want to see the commander of this facility." He pointed to the tents in the distance.

"He is not available. You need to turn back." Besides being demanding, the MP was also unyielding. He stayed on his bike in front of the car and was not about to move.

"Put the car in gear and flatten this bastard," the Captain ordered. Harold hesitated a moment too long, however, three seconds later the motorcycle was a wreck. The cop had dropped it just in time, jumping to safety. While Harold backed up, Alex got out and tried to engage the driver.

The MP took a single look at the Tatar and was sprinting back towards the road. "Let him run," smiled Pajari.

"I didn't see any regiment or battalion insignia on his uniform." Harold was done pushing the bike off the road, waiting for Alex to take his seat.

"That's why I ordered you to run him down. If I am right, we have a rogue operation in front of us."

He was correct. The tents were full of American food and assorted supplies. In a way it was kind of eerie because not a single soldier or officer was anywhere to be seen.

"I guess we can take whatever we want." Pajari looked around the first row of tents that stood right alongside the river. He didn't see anything he liked, however, in the second row of four tents he discovered some boxes marked 'Spam'. He motioned to Alex to load a few into the car.

"I don't expect to find any weapons, but let's check anyway." The group split up and rummaged through the remaining tents. The Captain had been right; besides the food they found tools and three tents with assorted lightweight medical supply cartons, but no weapons.

"How come there is no one around?" Harold was more than just curious. He wondered if there was a way to divert some of the food to the hungry civilian population.

"Oh, make no mistake, the thieves are around and I would bet that Alex already knows where they are hiding." The Captain followed the Tatar who looked repeatedly up and down the river. When they reached the car, Alex reached under the seat bench and retrieved, to Harold's surprise, a machine pistol. He hadn't even known that they had an automatic weapon on board.

"Back to the main thoroughfare and don't stop for anybody."

Harold was only too glad to follow the Captain's orders; Alex's unusual behavior was warning enough. But nothing happened. Within a few minutes they were back in formation with the other vehicles, avoiding the many damaged tanks alongside the road.

"What is a rogue operation?" Harold wanted to know.

"I'll give you the short version," Pajari explained. "The Americans have been supplying us for years. Not only vehicles and planes and weapons, but also with tools and food. Now that we don't need the stuff for the fighting troops, our officers are busy diverting the goodies for their own benefit."

"Isn't there an accounting in place?"

"Yes, there is. But, you have seen yourself all the different troop movements. Until we are able to restore some order there are ample opportunities for an enterprising officer to enrich himself."

"That is not what I meant. I know that there is a lot of confusion in your supply movements but what I am asking is in regard to the Americans. Don't you have to account to them?"

"The Americans?" laughed the captain. "They are like children. All they want is a pat on the back and they are happy. Anyway, their shipments during the last year have been more or less for political reasons."

When Pajari saw the questioning look in Harold's eyes he added: "Mind you, I don't really understand the Americans. It seems to me that these people need to feel good about their contributions. They are so rich that they don't give a crap about accounting."

"What about repayment?"

"You have amusing worries, Harold. Once you understand our system you will notice that repayment is not exactly one of our prime objectives."

"So, you think that Kommissar Godunov will be intrigued by our discovery?" Harold tried to steer his questions away from the Americans. He didn't understand the cavalier attitude of the Captain.

"Maybe. The medical supplies are certainly of value. On the other hand, we are happy to let the food diversions slide. The less we interfere, the higher the moral of our troops."

They followed the signs to the city headquarters and when they arrived it was too late to meet with the commander. After a meal consisting of several cans of Spam, they settled down in one of the empty rooms of a former school. The windows were broken and the doors had all been burned as firewood during the past winter. A cold spring wind was howling on and off throughout the building and the team was glad when the sun came up.

During the morning meeting with the commander, a colonel, Harold learned a whole lot more about the wide ranging powers of the various supply officers. At first he had a difficult time understanding the hard accent of the commander but once his ear got used to it, he was able to decipher that the administration was very well informed about various tent cities. Apparently there were quite a few of them.

Not only did the military headquarters know about their locations but based upon the words Harold understood, they did more than just tolerate them.

In a way, Harold admired the ingenious, but very effective scheme. Instead of coordinating the difficult task of supplying the various troops, the military administration had opted to turn a blind eye toward the virtual disappearance of the American relief transports. It saved them work and man-hours.

Depending upon the individual officer's talents, whole trains filled with vehicles and weapons were rerouted to the near and far east and the contents were either sold or bartered. Harold gathered that this kind of free enterprise was a very competitive activity among the officers who were old enough to retire, provided of course that some very high ranking officials received their fair share.

The more he listened, the more some of the recent happenings seemed to make sense. At one point in the rapid conversation between the Captain and the Colonel, he thought he heard a reference to General Berzarin who apparently had refused to play ball. He was unable to ascertain the identity of the final winner; however, Berzarin was the undisputed loser.

Just by listening and without any questions on his part he quickly became educated on the current events. The most interesting item, for him, was the fact that none of the Russian troops were actually being withdrawn. And while he could not discern the underlying reason, all indications pointed towards the opposite. The colonel remarked that the tanks along the Oder River would be battle ready within a few weeks.

Harold wondered why he was privileged to attend the meeting. While all the topics of discussion were new to him, he guessed that they were nothing but business as usual for the officers.

As the meeting ended, the Colonel handed the Captain a shoulder pouch. "Travel safe and give my regards to the Kommissar."

Harold had assumed that Pajari would transfer the documents into his briefcase which was always lying on the rear seat. However, the Captain draped the leather straps of the bag over his shoulder and didn't take it off when he sat down in the

PARTNERS TO A DEGREE

car.

"Let me see the German maps." Pajari studied first his temporary and rudimentary military road maps and then compared them with the old maps which Harold had secured in Berlin.

"Let's try to drive back on the west side of the Oder River," he instructed Harold, who complied and followed a German road sign out of Stettin. According to the maps there were only secondary roads winding between the farmlands on this side of the river and in the direction they needed to go in order to reach Potsdam.

At first he didn't like their slow progress but then he welcomed it. The longer it took to reach their destination the more chances he had to somehow fudge the letter into the pouch.

After a while it became clear that Pajari was searching for something along the railroad lines leading to Stettin. True to his latest resolutions, Harold resisted the impulse to ask questions. Instead he concentrated to figure out what the Captain was actually looking for.

"Pull up over there." It was the third or fourth time that Pajari ordered Harold to stop and they were still at least two hours away from Potsdam.

Pajari got out and made some notes as he inspected five railroad wagons standing abandoned on a designated spur leading to a destroyed yard. One other spur connected to a loading dock located right on the river's edge. The Captain had left his courier pouch on the seat but by the time Harold was aware of it and got his letter out of his pocket it was too late. Whatever Pajari was looking for he must have found it and he came back looking very satisfied. "These wagons are almost too good to be true. They are empty and clean besides being lockable."

To Harold's surprise the Captain opened the pouch from the Colonel and dumped all the documents on the backseat. "Help me sort through this mess. I am looking for a letter addressed to the military railroad commander in Berlin."

He reached for his own briefcase and retrieved a document which he compared with his notes from the train. "I have all the active transports listed. Unless we find a report to the railway headquarters, I have to assume that this train is not documented."

Harold could only guess why this would be important to the Captain. "Sorry that I cannot help you. You have not taught me to read Russian." He was unable to make heads or tails out of the Cyrillic letters.

Pajari nodded to himself as he arranged the paperwork in several lots. "Just place them back in the order I hand them to you." After the last letter was back in the pouch, Harold closed the snap lock. While the Captain had been concentrating on the individual documents, Harold had been able to successfully insert Godunov's letter.

"I can't help speculating, what good is a train without a locomotive?" He wondered aloud.

"You can always steal a locomotive. If the bribe is large enough you can also recruit an engineer. You will have to learn to think bigger, much bigger."

"Bigger?" echoed Harold.

"Yes, bigger. However, after you think big you have to back it up with action. Otherwise your thinking is nothing but daydreaming."

Pajari liked to use every possible opportunity to teach Harold in any way he could. "Look at it this way, Harold, everyone around you wishes for something or has some vision of achievement. In order to accomplish more than the next guy, you simply have to think bigger and then act to attain your vision. It's not that complicated, unless you choose to think that way."

Harold's brain did double time. First he translated the Russian words into German and then he strived to comprehend the advice in coherent manner. "It cannot be that easy," he objected, just in case he missed something.

"But, it is, Harold. The bigger you think and act, the less competition you have. On the other hand, the smaller you think and act, the harder it is to succeed, simply because you compete with the masses." The Captain hoped that some of his counsel would stick in the boy's mind and was pleasantly surprised at Harold's grasp in regard to the situation at hand.

"I think, I understand. So you fill the empty wagons, over there, with the goodies from the tent city, bribe a locomotive driver to reroute his engine and then drive the whole load to a destination where you are able to obtain the largest reward, or profit, if you will," Harold summarized his lesson.

"Very good, Harold. But how do you suppose we can move the goods from the tent city to this train? We would need several trucks, which we don't have, just to fill a single rail wagon."

"If you take care of the loc driver, I will bring the goods to the rail cars," Harold announced. He was a fast learner and thinking big seemed easy enough to give it an immediate try.

"And, what about the current owners of the tents?" Pajari probed Harold's mind.

"Hmm, at first blush a simple solution comes to mind. You could offer to them the transportation they need and split the profits." Harold thought that this was a definite possibility.

"Share, Harold, share, not split. Share means we give them a part of the profits. Maybe 25 percent but no more. Split, on the other hand, indicates that we would be willing to give them a full 50 percent," Pajari answered, elaborating on his lesson. In reality however, he was not thinking about sharing at all. "How long would it take you to transport the merchandise to the train?" He wanted to know.

"One day to organize and one night for the transfer would do it." Harold was already working on a plan. All he had to do was to entice knowledgeable locals to operate one or two of the river barges which he had seen on the previous day. The rest would be easy. The loading dock with the railroad spur was down river from the tent city. This would also track with his idea about sharing a little of the food with some lucky local residents.

"How many boxes of food will this cost me?" The Captain was not a mind reader, but he expected some kind of a price.

"We might need five to ten people. You might wish to give each of them two boxes of food." Harold figured that this would be more than adequate compensation for one night of work.

"Alright, Harold. After I make my delivery to the Marshal I will met with Kommissar Godunov to discuss this operation. If he gives his approval, we should be able to start on it within the next two days."

Sixteen

Pajari had been a little optimistic in his time estimate. It took four days until Harold was called to attend a meeting with the Kommissar and the Captain. In the meantime he had been busy studying the Cyrillic alphabet. He had no problems with the thirty three letters because the pronunciation was similar to the German language. Each letter was pronounced as it was spelled; however, the numerals were confusing because they were also represented by letters. He decided to shelf them until Pajari had the time to assist him.

"Tell me exactly how you intend to bring the merchandise to the railroad spur." Godunov spoke Russian to test Harold's progress.

"I saw several river barges near the town of Gartz. This is upriver but not very far from the tents. I should find a handful of people who are capable of floating the barges first to the depot and then down to the rail line." Harold's Russian had improved to the point that he could talk without resorting to German words. Godunov was pleased to notice, but not too happy about the answer.

"A handful of people are not nearly enough to load all the boxes first on the boat and then on the wagons. You will need to revise your initial plan." He looked at the Captain who scratched his head.

"I was under the impression that I was only to supply the method of transportation," Harold interjected.

"How big of an operation is this anyhow? Does it even make

sense for us to get involved?" Godunov was still addressing Pajari.

"Yes, it does. One of the tents is filled with boxes of the latest American miracle drug called Penicillin. This alone can net us a fortune," the Captain answered enthusiastically.

"Good, then we proceed in our usual manner." Godunov realized immediately the value of the rare penicillin. He envisioned in his mind new opportunities to broaden his exchange transactions. Actually, the cartons of medicine could be broken up into relatively smaller packages and used as door openers to new trading channels. In any event, they were much easier to hide and to transport than weapons or vehicles. The more he thought about it, the more he liked the idea.

"You and Harold leave immediately to secure the locals who know the river and how to operate a barge. Make certain that you reach the tent depot tomorrow evening; preferably shortly after it gets dark."

The Captain got up. "I assume that we are only after the medical supplies. This way we can offer the food as reward to the barge crew." He wanted to clarify the mission.

"Exactly, bring sufficient people to assure a speedy transfer. I will have the site secured by sunset tomorrow."

The Kommissar was already at the door. He needed to round up his regular detail but also wanted to meet with Marshal Zhukov before he left for the Oder River. He always tried to give the appearance of working in tandem with the military commander.

The Captain did the driving and Harold kept on asking questions about the Cyrillic numeral letters. In spite of Pajari's best efforts, he found them difficult to understand. He decided that he needed to make some notes for himself.

*****

They reached the small town of Gartz in the early afternoon. However, securing a barge was a much more complicated task than Harold had anticipated. For one thing, the barges he had seen a few days ago were virtually unusable. For whatever reason or none at all, they had all been sabotaged by the SS before the Russians had crossed the river. And even if they had been operational, they would have been useless due to the broken-down remains of a bridge blocking any downstream river traffic. Harold decided to ask for the German city supervisor for advice.

Gartz was an old but tiny town without an active city office. It took him some time to find the house of someone who was described to him as a city manager. His name was Edelberg and Harold guessed that he was at least in his late sixties. After the first few words of introduction it seemed that the city manager didn't like the German teenager in the Russian uniform. The giant Tatar standing right behind the boy didn't help either. He could also see a Russian officer in a car, parked across the street.

"Sorry, all you have to do is to look at the harbor and you can see for yourself that I am unable to help you." Edelberg had listened to Harold's plea without inviting him into his home. He looked at the boy through his rimless glasses which he now took off.

"So, even the possibility of obtaining food for your hospital or elderly does not trigger any solution?" Harold was not giving up.

"No," Edelberg was about to close the door in Harold's face when his attitude changed. "Food? Did you say food? What kind of food? Do you have it with you?"

"No, I don't have it with me. But I can offer you canned meat if you help me," Harold answered anxiously.

"If you can't show it to me, you don't have any." The door was about to close again.

"What is it with you grownups that you use us if it is convenient for you, but you never listen to us?" Harold decided on a different tactic.

"Alright, I am listening, but only for a minute. Make the most of it." The city manager seemed to be serious about the time limit.

Harold had a sudden idea and said something to Alex who turned and went to the car and returned with a can of spam in his hand. Edelberg reached for the canned meat without knowing what it was. "You did this within sixty seconds and without talking. I am impressed. Come in, but your Mongol has to stay outside."

He took a step backward, opening the door for Harold and Alex entered without invitation. It was not entirely clear if the city manager liked it, but Alex was already in the house and Edelberg was unable to do anything about it. "Your friend is a bit

PARTNERS TO A DEGREE

aggressive," he managed to remark.

The door had opened into a very small hallway and Edelberg led the way into the kitchen. He opened the can and smelled the meat. Apparently it met his approval. Alex stood ignored at the door while Edelberg motioned to Harold to take a seat.

"You need some advice my boy. Next time show what you have to offer before you start asking for help. You will get faster results."

To Harold's astonishment he produced three dishes and divided the meat equally. "You said that you had some more, right?" He proceeded to offer a chair and a dish to Alex.

Harold nodded "Much more and many different items."

"You have my attention. Start at the beginning." Edelberg enjoyed the meat while he studied his two guests.

"You can have several truckloads of food by tomorrow night," Harold started, following the city manager's advice to keep the enticement in the forefront.

"Go on" Edelberg was now all ears.

"I need help to transport a specific load of items for a distance of about ten miles down the river."

"How heavy are the items? Are we talking about weapons or machinery?" Edelberg knew that the Russians had started to disassemble whole factories which they were shipping east. He wanted no part of it.

"No, I am talking about boxes and cases, maybe twenty-five pounds each." Harold was not volunteering more than necessary.

"Great God in heaven, why have you been asking for a barge?"

All of a sudden the city manager showed genuine interest in the boy's story. He was well aware that many of the Russian officers acted in their own self-interest. It was, however, new to him that they resorted to using German boys to further their individual agenda.

"Because I noticed them when we passed your town on the opposite side of the river."

"Good enough. What was your name, again?"

"Harold will suffice."

"Alright, Harold, now, to the truckloads of food. Do you have trucks available?"

"No, this was another reason for a barge. I planned to have the crew load up the vessel with the food and somehow hide it or pull it back up the stream. I have seen this done before." He had actually never seen it, but he had read about it.

"Well, this was a miscalculation on your part. There are no healthy men to serve as a crew and the work would be too strenuous for women."

In spite of his words, Edelberg still sounded optimistic. "When do you need our help?"

"Tomorrow evening would be perfect. If there are any ranching roads on this side of the river I can take you there tomorrow morning to show you the temporary depot and the railroad dock."

The city manager smiled at Harold's answer. "Well, consider your problem solved. I know where the tents are and I also know where the rail spur is located. Before the war we transferred potatoes from the barges to the freight trains."

He got up to open the front door and had another question. "Where do you intend to spend the night? There are only three of you, right?" He gestured to the car which had not moved. Pajari could be patient to a fault.

"I was hoping for an empty room in your school house." Harold had not even thought about sleep.

"Nonsense. You can stay in my place. I am a widower and live alone."

Before Harold could accept the offer the city manager added: "I would accept some tobacco as payment."

"Of course, we will share with you whatever we have."

He crossed the street to the waiting Captain to give him the good news about their quarters for the night. "What about a barge?" Pajari was piqued.

"According to the city manager *our problem is solved.*"

"'What does that mean?"

"I am not real sure. However, I know that Herr Edelberg is greedy enough to make good on his promise." Harold was pretty confident that the city manager already had a plan in mind.

"You better ask him tomorrow morning, if only to have some kind of a backup in place. I would hate to face the Kommissar with empty hands." Pajari was adamant and Harold had to agree that

PARTNERS TO A DEGREE

he felt the same way.

*****

Sleep came late for him. He rolled around on the carpet in the small living room and dreamed up all kinds of possible scenarios. A few days ago the Captain had advised him to think big. He could not imagine anything bigger than a barge, but, the barges on hand did not provide an answer.

The next morning Harold appreciated Herr Edelberg's local knowledge. He showed him access roads close to the river and all the way to the rail spur. Along the trip, the Captain pressed him for some kind of assurance as to his ability to provide the needed transport.

"All I can tell you is that I will get your selected packages to the freight wagon because Harold promised me all the food in the depot," the city manager replied and pointed to the tents across the river. "I am also given to understand that there will be no guards on duty after we load your railroad car."

"Correct," the Captain assured him.

"Then let's go back. I have plenty of work to do before the evening. I'll be exactly below your tents right after dark. Promise."

Pajari looked dubious at Harold who shrugged his shoulders. "He is definitely motivated. I trust him," he said in Russian.

The Captain was not too convinced and decided to discuss the vague promise of the city manager with the Kommissar before they took any action.

*****

They crossed the river on a shaky new pontoon bridge and drove along the main thoroughfare, hoping to see Godunov's team at the turn off to the tent depot. Harold attempted to count the repaired Russian tanks which stood in seemingly endless rows on the grounds next to the road. He gave up on the second try .There were far too many.

Besides the very familiar T34s he noticed two models he had not seen before. One was an extremely strange, almost ugly looking slightly smaller vehicle. The Captain told him that it was called a T60 and that it was not in production anymore.

"What are they doing here, after the war?" Harold wondered

if the tank might be used in the upcoming victory parades he had heard about.

"Why are you looking at the antiquated models? Have you seen the JS tanks over there?" Pajari pointed to the other side of the road where Harold could see, row after row, the famous Joseph Stalin Panzers.

He had seen some of them during the battle in Berlin, but what amazed him was the fact that the tanks, parked in a field, looked practically new. As far as he could determine they had never been involved in combat. There was no indication of any defects or repairs.

It had been only a few days since Harold had passed this place but it looked different now. On the previous trip he had missed the real tank crews. All he had seen were the repair companies and now they were almost gone. Instead, there were new campsites after campsites alongside the road. Wherever he looked, he saw fresh looking tank crews in unsoiled uniforms. Even Alex noted the change and pointed repeatedly at the shiny new outfits of the soldiers.

Then, within a few miles of the crossroad to the river, the camps of the new troops disappeared. Instead they now saw several MPs on motorcycles patrolling the stretch close to the turn off. The traffic moved at a pretty fast clip and Pajari motioned to Harold to pass the turnoff and to keep going.

"Turn around, a little further up the road."

As soon as Harold had followed the order, he had a MP showing up next to him. While he first frantically waved at Harold to stop, he did the opposite when Harold rolled to a halt, right at the junction.

"Continue driving. You are not permitted to stop at this place," shouted the police officer.

"I stop where I please," answered Pajari showing his star emblem as he got out of the car. The motorcycle cop glanced at the star and without saying another word he parked his bike in the center of the road leading to the river. He just stayed in the seat, looking up and down the main highway. Apparently he had specific orders of what to do and he was getting nervous.

"Who is in command of this outfit?" Pajari asked in a friendly tone trying to diffuse any possible conflict before it started. He waved in the general direction of the tent compound.

"It is a colonel. I don't know his name. I have orders to stop any visitors." The cop answered slowly and then relaxed when another MP turned off the road and parked next to him. Within a few minutes Pajari's car was surrounded by five motorcycles.

"Keep your hands off your weapons. You will be dead soon enough. No need for any haste." Pajari casually waved at Alex who stood up to reveal his size and one of the officers gasped as the giant Tatar slowly moved in his direction.

"Listen very carefully," the Captain showed his identification for all the cops to see. "These are your new orders. Get lost as fast as possible and if you see your commanding officer tell him that I am here to arrest him. Now move!"

For a short moment, Harold had the impression that the cops were deaf. Nobody moved, except Alex who had reached the first bike. He ignored the cop and with a sharp pull he ripped out the fuel line below the tank of the bike. As the gasoline trickled out, the policeman decided to run. It was too late, Alex was faster. He tripped him and then grabbing him at his feet he swirled him around. With a sickening sound the policeman's head connected with the bumper of the car. He didn't get up. There was no blood or visible injury. He just didn't move anymore.

Harold had thought that the other cops would offer some kind of resistance, but Alex's actions and the fear of the GPU were overwhelming. Within a heartbeat they scattered down the highway. However, one brave soul took off in the direction of the tents.

Alex pulled the motionless body of the MP to the side of the road and then dragged the disabled motorbike on top of him. The fuel was still leaking out of the tank and Harold feared that the Captain would give an order to flick a match at it. But Pajari was satisfied and called to Alex to return to the car.

"Enough is enough, no need for cruelty," Pajari remarked as if he was a mind reader. "The MP who went to the tents will spread the word. I would be surprised to see any guards when we get down there."

It took another hour until Godunov arrived with his team. They arrived in two trucks and Harold noticed that there were only a few regular soldiers among them. Most of them were sergeants with a junior lieutenant in charge. He had never seen any of them before and it almost looked as if they had never been under the command of the Kommissar. He speculated that they were dispatched from the new city commander of Berlin.

    He was wrong. As he found out later, they were a special guard unit for political officers. Godunov knew how to protect himself.

Seventeen

"Have you seen any MPs along the road?" Pajari was eager to know.

"No. Not a single one." Godunov was certain.

"Good. Just to be sure, I recommend we leave one of the trucks with a few men here at the intersection," Pajari suggested.

"Fine with me, you are in command of this operation." He looked at the sky. "It will be dark soon. Will your barge be on time?"

Godunov asked because he wondered how this could even be possible. He had seen the ruins of the bridges and felt they would impede any kind of river traffic.

"Ask Harold." Pajari didn't feel like elaborating. He was busy selecting the men who would stay behind with the truck.

"Yes, he will show up on time." Harold didn't know what else to say and hoped that he was right.

Just as Pajari had predicted, there was not a sentry in sight as the team advanced towards the river. The MP had done a good job of alerting the camp to the presence of a political officer. None of the guards, or whoever was in charge, was crazy enough to hang around.

It looked to Harold as if some of the food boxes were gone. The first row of tents were nearly empty of canned goods and some larger crates with tools had been added.

"I hope there is enough food left to reward the transportation crews," he remarked to Pajari and then realized that he had spoken too early. The second row of tents was overflowing with the American provisions. There must have been some reason to shift the merchandise around.

"We just made it in time," announced the Captain. "Whoever is running this operation is taking advantage of the disassembly of the German manufacturing plants. They are collecting and hoarding replacement parts of machines and tools." He was done examining the newly arrived merchandise.

"This is not a spur of the moment operation. They are planning to be in this business for a long time," he declared.

"How can you tell?" Harold wanted to learn.

"All the factories we are shipping to Russia will eventually be in need of pertinent tools and special replacement units. We don't have the knowledge to build them. Whoever owns or controls the supplements will be sitting nicely."

It made sense to Harold that the food operation was a short time venture, if just for the fact that the food shortage would not last forever.

"If you don't have the knowledge, who will operate the machines and factories once they are reassembled?" Harold asked of Godunov who had joined them.

"We will deport any engineer or expert we need from Germany. We will also process the POW transports to make sure that we don't send specialists to labor camps in Siberia."

Godunov's answer confirmed what Harold had heard on the streets. He had dismissed the bits and pieces of information as nothing but rumors and now recognized that he had been wrong. Besides the manpower and selected factories, Russia was also bent on removing the brainpower from Germany. He had no way of knowing if the Western Allies were doing the same or pursued likewise goals in their occupied territory.

Harold's thoughts were interrupted by a young German boy who appeared all of a sudden out of nowhere.

"I guess that you are Harold. Herr Edelberg sent me to tell you that we are ready." The boy seemed to be eleven or twelve years old. He addressed Harold without so much as even looking at the soldiers.

"You are right, I am Harold. What is your name and did Herr Edelberg bring a barge?"

"A barge? I don't know about a barge. My name is Bernd and I am here with my mother. Herr Edelberg is waiting for you by the river." The boy was eager to show the way.

Twilight was gone and the first stars made their appearance. Harold hesitated for a moment to look for Alex who had joined Godunov's team. They were busy combing the bushes around the tents to make sure all of the guards had abandoned the depot.

"Come on, Harold. My mother is waiting." Bernd was getting impatient.

"I hope you know where you are going. I can hardly see the next bush, let alone a path to the river." Harold stumbled behind the boy as well as he could.

"All we have to do is to walk downhill. The river cannot be on higher ground." Bernd seemed to be amused by the naivety of the city boy.

After a short walk the bushes gave way to an opening and Harold could see Herr Edelberg surrounded by dozens of women. There were also many children in Bernd's age group as well as some elderly men.

"I mobilized the river dwellers all the way down to the rail dock. We have over fifty small boats ready to move your shipment and also to receive the promised food," Edelberg said in a way of greeting. "Come on, I'll show you what we have." He proudly pointed to the shore. In spite of the darkness Harold could make out the contours of small rowboats and fishing vessels.

"This is much better than a barge. I am impressed." He could hear Godunov's deep voice behind him. He had not noticed that the Kommissar had followed him. "I guess that each boat could carry at least two hundred pounds?" Godunov continued. He could see that Harold was about to introduce him to Edelberg but he wanted no part of it.

"Don't mind me, I am only asking because I wonder how many boxes we will be able to load in each boat." His normally perfect German was all of a sudden a broken miss match interspersed with Russian phrases. Harold wondered what this was about, but decided to play along.

"This is Captain Pajari's second hand. He will oversee the details of the transportation." He waved first towards the Kommissar and then in the direction of Edelberg. "This is the German city manager of Gartz."

Edelberg wanted to say something but Godunov was already

going back to the depot. "We will form a fire brigade to get the cartons to the boats," Harold could hear him saying in Russian and translated it for the benefit of Edelberg.

A moment later Alex showed up with Captain Pajari right behind him. When the German women saw the hulk of the Tatar they flinched and if not for Harold, they would have surely taken off. However, Harold as well as Herr Edelberg was able to convince them that they had nothing to fear.

Alex was already carrying a box marked *Penicillin* and looked for a place to set it down. He saw that Bernd was beckoning him towards a fishing boat and after receiving an approving nod from Pajari he stashed the first carton onboard.

It took a few minutes to get the logistics figured out. Godunov's team selected the cargo and carried it to the shore where the women and the boys sorted it out by weight and loaded it into the boats. Pajari was to accompany the first larger boat to the railroad wagon but wanted to wait until all the medication boxes had reached the shore. He was greatly surprised at how many cartons fit on the individual little boats.

After the word came from Godunov that all the penicillin and the cartons with narcotics were gone, Harold counted thirty three loaded boats. He had kept a tally of the individual boxes, which numbered 240. He looked at the boats again and saw that they each carried between 7 and 8 boxes. That's about right, he thought to himself.

"Let's get the show on the road." Pajari wanted to shove off but was delayed by Edelberg who wanted to know about their reward.

"Walk up to the depot and help yourself," suggested Pajari who was anxious to leave.

"No. Can't do that, as this would amount to stealing and we might get shot." The city manager didn't know if the Captain was backing out of his promise or if he was just in a hurry to get going. He looked at Harold for some kind of assistance or reassurance, but he didn't need to worry. Godunov was already sending the first boxes with canned goods, which his team deposited on the shoreline. Within a short while there was more food on the shore than the remaining boats could carry.

"Not a problem," smiled Edelberg. "We have carts and horse

carriages standing by on the other side. We only need to cross the river a few times."

Pajari selected a few soldiers from Godunov's team to escort him in two additional boats and waved at Harold with a final order. "Meet me tomorrow morning at the railroad spur."

Harold understood and waved back. He stood next to Edelberg watching the action on the river.

There was not much of a current to speak of but the women and children propelled the boats anyhow with a remarkable speed down the river. Harold marveled at the cleverness of the crews. They tied the boats loosely together to prevent getting lost and due to the darkness, they were out of sight within a minute.

The remaining boat teams were no less inventive. The first boat crossed the river and pulled a long rope along. When the end of the rope appeared, Edelberg tied a second rope on and after a total of three ropes the first boat had reached the other side and turned immediately around. On the way back, it dragged a long sequence of ropes behind it.

The city manager tied the returned rope to the end of the first one, thereby establishing a loop. The rest was easy. When a boat was loaded, one of the children or women jumped in to hold on to the line and the remaining crews on the shore simply pulled the boats across the stream and back. Due to the slow running river they were able to do this with very little effort and at an astonishing speed. It was now just a task of loading the boats as fast as possible.

Shortly after midnight the last box of canned food was loaded.

"Thanks for everything and remember us whenever you need help again."

Edelberg walked up to Harold and shook his hand. He didn't know how to thank Alex who reached in his pocket and presented the city manager with a packet of cigarettes. He had found a whole carton of American Lucky Strike's which he had immediately appropriated for himself by placing it in their car. One of Godunov's team had observed him but was discouraged to object when Alex locked eyes with him.

Harold was pleased to see how fast the German civilians disappeared. Edelberg's boat was the last one to be pulled across the river and when Godunov's lieutenant showed up to see how things were going he was astonished that there was nothing for him to do.

"The Kommissar wants to see you," he said to Harold and looked longingly at the round cigarette in Alex's hand. The faint smell of American tobacco confirmed what was he was thinking.

"Alex, please share a cigarette with the lieutenant." Harold addressed Alex in his native tongue. He knew how much the Tatar disliked any Russian officer and he wanted to keep peace as long as possible.

"If you say so. But only one and the hero better say thank you." Alex shook a cigarette out of the pack and instead of offering the smoke to the lieutenant, he gave it to Harold.

"Don't mind my friend; he is usually a lot friendlier. Maybe he hurt himself carrying one of the boxes." Harold passed the cigarette to the officer who was surprised at the boy's language skills.

"Thank you, comrade." He was instinctively smart enough to look at the Tatar when he said it.

*****

"If you are able to find your way in the dark, I want you to take one of my sergeants and drive to the railroad dock and bring the Captain back to me in Berlin." Godunov had also made his way to the river and addressed Harold.

"I can take off as soon as you want me to." Harold walked back with the group and inspected the partially empty tents.

"Do you need any help with the remaining merchandise, Herr Godunov?"

"No. I thought of burning the tents down, however, I now know who is behind this scheme. It is a colonel and he will be only too willing to share a portion of his profit with me."

"How can you tell who is running this operation?" Harold had not seen any evidence pointing to a specific military unit.

"Habits, Harold. Habits are hard to break and will always give you away."

The Kommissar pointed to the crates of tools that stood in exact lines, lined up according to size.

"There is only one commanding officer I know of who is obsessed with order in everything he does. I suspect it is some

PARTNERS TO A DEGREE

kind of a mental disorder and I think they have a name for it." Godunov smiled to himself. "In any event, the poor fellow can't help himself."

The Kommissar's face turned serious as he faced Harold. "Don't ever develop any signature habits, Harold. Or at least be aware of them so you can break them. They will invariably betray you."

"Thank you, Herr Godunov. This is indeed valuable advice."

Harold was glad that the Kommissar had the unerring practice of teaching him at every opportunity. He had a momentary flashback of Karl who had always ironed his own shirts because his mother couldn't do it well enough. *Now there was a signature habit if there ever was one,* he smiled at the memory of his friend.

"This is sergeant Grigory. He will stay with the railroad wagon when you return with the Captain." Godunov was also ready to leave with his group. He gave some final instructions to the sergeant and then gathered his people to move out.

Harold used the temporary pontoon bridge again and then turned north on a secondary road. He had found a few fully-filled gasoline cans at the depot and knew that even if he made a slight mistake in his navigation, he would still have enough fuel to get to the loading dock and then back to Berlin.

The sergeant was sleeping on the rear seat and Alex helped Harold to stay awake by feeding him canned spam and from time to time, blowing cigarette smoke in his direction.

They reached the loading dock shortly after sunrise and when Harold rolled to a stop he didn't bother to get out of the car. He was dead tired and fell asleep with his head supported by the steering wheel.

"Move to the rear and keep on sleeping. I will drive us to Berlin." The sun was already on its way down when Pajari tried to get Harold out of the driver's seat.

"Where is everybody?" Harold had expected that the car would be crowded on their way back, but, there was only Alex who was filling the gas tank with one of the spare cans.

"I see only four wagons. Where is the fifth one?" Harold was now fully awake. He got out and looked at the railroad cars which seemed to be empty.

"The Kommissar had arranged for a locomotive and it was waiting for us when we arrived." Pajari motioned to Harold to come back to the car.

"And the boats and women and children?"

"They are all gone. It's over. Take a seat and let's go."

Harold felt almost guilty that he had slept through the final stage of the mission. The drive to Berlin was by now pretty much routine and when they reached the Kommissar's quarters it was dark again. Godunov had left a note for them advising them to meet up with him on the following day.

Harold had hoped to learn where the shipment of the medical supplies ended up, thereby possibly discovering the full scope of the Kommissar's network. He was disappointed when Godunov handed him a severely used dictionary and ordered him to stay in his room for the next three days to increase his Russian vocabulary. For about half of the days he was still taught by the Captain and for the other half, he buried himself in the book and in his notes.

He did as he had been ordered but he was not fully convinced this was a faster way to achieve a command of the Russian language. He much rather preferred being immersed in the day to day verbiage by actual contact with the different Russian soldiers. However, after the third day he realized that he was now able to read simple sentences. A feat he thoroughly enjoyed. An additional bonus was the fact that he learned useable words instead of adding to his already overflowing inventory of curses.

On the morning of the fourth day he was surprised when the Kommissar handed him an old German rucksack (backpack) and told him that they would be driving to Switzerland. Harold could easily see that the top of the rucksack was packed with used underwear and wondered what it might be covering up.

The rucksack weighed in excess of maybe twenty pounds and he doubted very much that he was carrying dirty laundry around.

He was not the only one to be surprised by the trip. Just before they took off with a Russian lieutenant at the wheel, Alex came running out of the building and without asking the Kommissar for permission, he took a seat next to Harold in the back of the American built Jeep.

Eighteen

"I wondered what kept him. Short of shooting him, I doubt that you are ever able to leave him behind," Godunov said in English and gave Alex an encouraging smile.

The Tatar grunted as if he understood and handed Harold a loaf of bread. It was still warm. Even the Kommissar had no idea how Alex always managed to get his hands on freshly baked goods.

Before they left Berlin, Godunov needed to visit the new city commander. It looked to Harold as if they had been expected. The Kommissar was hardly gone when he returned and placed another small satchel between Harold and Alex on the back seat.

Except for a short stop on the Elbe River where they crossed into the British and then to the American occupied territory, they traveled freely but slowly through southern Germany to the Swiss border.

Harold was baffled to see that most of the countryside as well as the cities in western and southern Germany were hardly damaged by the war. Every now and then he noted some evidence of air attacks but this was minimal and in stark contrast to the ruins of the devastated East Germany.

"It looks as if the Germans offered only minimal resistance to the British and American forces," Harold remarked when they neared the Swiss border the next morning.

"It may have been that you feared the Soviets more than the Americans, or that the major SS units were pulled back to defend Berlin," Godunov agreed. "We had to fight for every single bloody foot of your land and our casualties, compared to the Western

Allies, proves it," he added.

"Do you have a tally already?" Harold asked.

"We are still counting. Our present estimates are that we lost more than seven million soldiers, not to mention our civilian losses which also numbers into the millions."

"What about the Western Allies. Do you have any figures?"

"Not really, because the Americans are still fighting the Japanese but we guess that the western combined casualties are less than one half of a million."

"This is news to me. I thought that the war was over. I didn't know that the Japanese are still fighting." Harold was surprised to hear this.

"Oh yes, they most certainly are. We will have a meeting of the super powers within a week or so in Potsdam and I would not be surprised if we declare war on the Japanese."

"Are you saying that Churchill and Truman will come to Potsdam?" Harold was thinking of the massive Soviet troops he had seen last week between Berlin and Poland. He had difficulty believing that the western leaders would not choose a more neutral and secure meeting place.

"Premiere Joseph Stalin will be there too. The conference will be held to determine the future of Germany." The Kommissar wanted to add something but the driver had stopped at the Swiss border control station. While Godunov produced documents identifying himself and his associates, Harold noted that the Swiss border control paid no attention to him. However they eyed Alex as if he came from another planet.

If he ever had any misgivings about the Kommissar's clout, they vanished when the guards made no attempt to examine their luggage.

It seemed as if they were ready to wave them through when Godunov made a request. He was speaking English, so that the driver could not understand what he was saying, but Harold understood that the Kommissar wanted to leave the lieutenant at the control station. He told the border agents that he would return within twenty-four hours to pick him up and it seemed to Harold that his request was not so unusual. The Swiss border patrol offered the driver a small room in their station and Godunov explained to him that there was nothing he could do about it. He

PARTNERS TO A DEGREE

didn't have the right credentials for him and the Swiss were nitpickers and that was that.

It was clear to Harold this was not the first time that Godunov had been in Switzerland. He knew where he was going and drove with confidence along the narrow mountain roads to the small town of Aarau.

"I will introduce you to an old friend of mine. Should anything ever happen to me and you need help, he is the man to see," Godunov told Harold as he stopped in front of a small house. A bronze sign next to the entrance announced that they were at the financial service office of Bruno Graf.

The introduction as well as their visit was short but very friendly. Bruno looked like a man in his late forties. He was dressed in an old-fashioned suit, spoke fluent Russian and offered his visitors some homemade sausage. The Kommissar gathered the backpacks and disappeared with Herr Graf into another room. Shortly thereafter, he returned with the same satchels. The bags were somewhat lighter now and Harold would bet that the same underwear was still in his backpack.

"What is your father's birth date?" Herr Graf asked, taking a small notebook from his pocket together with a fountain pen, ready to write. .

"04/10/03" Answered Harold.

"This will be your access number for anything the Kommissar has designated or will designate for you to know and to have."

Bruno Graf penned the number neatly in his book and asked Harold to repeat it once more.

"Good. You will not forget it and I have it written down." Herr Graf could see that Harold seemed to have a question on his lips.

"Don't worry; we are a family business in the third generation. If I am not here anymore, my son or another family member will know your number and be able to help you."

It was the first time that Harold had met a private banker and in spite of the informal surroundings he was duly impressed. Later on in life he would meet a few more people of the same ilk in different places and different nations, but the little Swiss house always stuck in his mind as the most trustworthy.

"How come you trust a Swiss gnome with your affairs instead of a Russian banker?" he asked on the way back to the border.

"Because you cannot trust a Russian or any other banker as much as a Swiss," was the short answer.

"But why?" insisted Harold.

"Several reasons. For one thing they have privacy laws in Switzerland which are like no others in the world. In every other nation, the state controls or has access to your personal financial information."

Harold remembered that his father had told him that the wealthy Jewish people had taken their gold and other valuables to Switzerland, long before Hitler's purge began.

"Please, give me another reason," Harold probed.

"Alright, the Swiss are smarter business people."

"Can you give me an example?" Harold pressed further.

"Well, there are many, but here is a simple one." Godunov enjoyed the questions from his protégé. "Take for instance the Germans. They are smart people and built a great car, the Mercedes Benz. Or, take the British engineers; they built the famous Rolls Royce. Now, in order to build these cars they need large properties to build their factories and, when the cars are finished, once again they need vast real estate to store their inventory. They need acres of land just to park, let's say, one thousand cars." Godunov paused for a moment to assure himself that he was still on the correct road to the border.

"Now take the Swiss watchmaker. His production facility is extremely small compared to an automobile factory. He is able to produce a watch of equal value to a car, in a single room in his home. And his inventory? He can store hundreds of watches pinned on the wall of his room. Should he wish to store more, he can simply lean a board against the wall and double his inventory space. I didn't even mention the difference in shipping costs. There is no comparison."

Harold was fascinated by Godunov's example.

"How do you account for the Swiss intelligence?" he wanted to know.

The Kommissar shrugged his shoulders. "For my money, I guess that the Swiss are forced to think. Their country is not only small but it is also not level. They could not compete with agricultural nations who have plenty of area. Our Ukrainian farmers have practically unlimited acreage for our wheat fields and the American cotton growers, they also have plenty of level land. Switzerland is a very small mountain country and was relatively poor when the nations evolved. In order to survive they needed to use their brain as it was intended to be used. So they did.

Here is another example. They don't grow a single cocoa bean and still produce some of the best tasting chocolate in the world. Then they added confidentiality and banking laws which now benefit and serve not only individuals but other nations as well."

They had reached the control station on the Swiss/German border and reclaimed their driver who, in spite of the Swiss hospitality, was glad to see them. It was getting late in the day and Godunov decided to visit an American military facility somewhere along the Rhine River to spend the night.

"Don't leave without sharing breakfast with us," an American officer invited them.

The next morning when he opened the door to a dining room, Harold was overwhelmed by the assortment of the American breakfast which was served buffet style. He was aghast when he saw some American soldiers helping themselves more than once and the greatest surprise was the orange juice which stood in tall glass carafes on the tables.

"How is this possible? Are they squeezing the fruit and throwing the remainder away? Do the Americans really realize how wealthy they are?" he asked of Godunov who was also mesmerized.

"I don't know," he confessed. "I studied for a while in Paris and the French are happy to have toast and jelly in the morning. The Polish and the Russians are glad when they have a choice of bread or fish. I am not familiar with the British but I doubt that they are as affluent as the Americans. But no, I think the American soldiers take it for granted to be able to eat every day and then as much as they want. I doubt very much that they comprehend how rich they are."

Harold silently observed Alex who stood in wonderment in

front of all the assorted food and then started to sample the bacon. Harold could hear him mutter something he didn't understand. "What is he saying?" he asked Godunov.

"He is wondering what kind of holiday the Americans are celebrating." Godunov smiled and encouraged Alex to help himself to some of the other items.

Harold understood what the Tatar was thinking. He, himself, had never seen a display of food like this. And orange juice? He had never heard of it. He had never eaten an orange in his life; however, his friend Karl had told him once that that he had received an orange for Christmas.

They thoroughly enjoyed the hospitality of the Americans and took their time before continuing their trip.

During the drive back to Berlin Harold kept unusually quiet. He could not understand why people who were so obviously wealthy would come all the way over the great ocean to conquer his homeland. He somehow understood the Russians because Germany had invaded their country and they most certainly had an ax to grind. But, the Americans had far more to eat than the Germans ever had. Their uniforms were immaculate, their footwear was excellent and their trucks and cars were new and shiny. What could they possibly gain in Germany?

And then he remembered what the Russian officers had told him about the atrocities the SS had committed. All the stories he had heard, but doubted before, must have been true.

He thought back to the instructors in the elite cadet school he had attended and added bits and pieces he had heard until his head hurt from all the different pieces of information.

"I am slowly starting to understand why there will be a war crime tribunal coming up. I just don't understand how and why my father got involved."

Godunov looked up with a puzzled expression. He had been calculating how long it might take to obtain his part of the profit from the diversion of the penicillin and if he needed to make another trip to Switzerland. The politburo in Moscow had ordered him to stay close to Marshall Stalin during the upcoming Potsdam conference. He was usually very good at arranging a change in his orders, however, to stay close to Stalin had its own rewards. In a way he was looking forward to obtaining the latest information regarding the inevitable war with Japan. His contacts in Asia were experts in converting critical information into gold.

"What are you talking about?" he asked Harold.

"Well, I can see now that Hitler and his regime must have been the reason that a country like America felt it was their duty to invade us. But, my father was part of the food supply system in Berlin. No matter how I look at it, I am unable to associate him with any criminal activity." Harold's thoughts had worked themselves into a loop and he tried to clear his head.

"Since I heard from Major Tesslov about the possible dismissal of criminal charges against your father, I sent another request to the prison commandant to release your father into my custody. I told you before that I have no leverage at the Allied prison facility but there is always the possibility that my persistence will pay off."

The Kommissar had misunderstood Harold's remark. "Thank you, Herr Godunov. I didn't know that you were still pursuing the release of my father and I was only trying to make sense of all the confusing things that I saw during the past months."

Harold continued to evaluate and then reevaluate his thoughts and it was to him as if he experienced a transformational awakening. By the time the car crossed the Elbe River he had reached some new conclusions. Most of all he was now more than ever convinced that he had done the right thing by accepting Godunov's offer.

Even if his father was freed tomorrow, he could not picture himself staying in Germany. Too many people and teachers he had trusted had lied to him. Leaders he had looked up to were now awaiting trial as war criminals. He had seen youngsters his own age being executed by the SS because they were retreating from the enemy. It didn't matter that the perpetrators were wearing the black uniforms with the SS insignia. They were still his countrymen, engaged in outright murder.

Maybe his decision to tie his life to Godunov was not the wisest move, considering all the self-serving actions of the Kommissar, but for the time being he was happy with his choice. His contemplations ended when the car pulled up at Godunov's quarters.

While Harold went to sleep, Godunov had some additional business to take care of. He checked his messages, which had piled up since he was gone. The first one of any importance was from Marshal Zhukov informing him that he was now an assigned member of a special inquiry board regarding the death of General Berzarin.

Godunov smiled when he read the order. He had triggered this request himself when he had asked Harold to sneak a fake letter into the document pouch carried by Captain Pajari. For one thing, Harold had been right when he thought that the Kommissar might be testing his abilities. But, this experiment was only a byproduct of the far more elaborate scheme which Godunov had dreamed up during the past few years.

In essence he had created a bogus entity within the State police. An entity that in reality did not exist. He started it when he felt that he needed, from time to time, an innocent third party influence or even assistance. In the beginning, he wrote diminutive letters of opinion and recommendation and sent them to different military commanders, always careful to leave his name out of it. He signed them with phony titles of nonexistent people. His method worked like a charm because none of the military officers would ever think of questioning a favorable comment from what seemed to be a political big wig.

Over the years and especially lately, he added to his ingenious plot. While his initial objective had been to secure himself a secure and comfortable retirement, he had changed his goals since Germany had surrendered. He could clearly see that Stalin was on his way to creating communistic satellite states around the Russian borders in Europe. He could envision himself as the political chief in charge of one or, if possible, all of these states. In due time he could conceivably advance to the very top of the almighty secret state police. To further his new goal and to add authenticity, he started to sign the papers with the names and titles of real people. People he knew who were on the politburo black list. Due to his inside track, he knew which officials would fall out of grace with Stalin and would therefore either be sent to forced labor camps or simply eliminated. None of these former party officials would or could ever be questioned.

He had written the phony letter to Marshal Zhukov to be

PARTNERS TO A DEGREE

assigned to the team which was to investigate corruptions. From now on he was able to watch his own back.

Godunov was satisfied with the results of his actions and turned his attention to a message from his daughter who informed him that she was released from active duty. She was safe at home and recovering from her ordeal in Potsdam.

Nineteen

The next morning started with Captain Pajari announcing to the Kommissar that he had knowledge of a transport train that contained original machinery from Junkers (a German airplane manufacturer).

For one reason or another, the fully loaded train stood abandoned on a deserted factory spur close to the city of Dessau in the Russian occupied territory of Germany.

"What do you wish to do about it?" Pajari wanted to know if the Kommissar had any desire to reroute this train for his own benefit.

"I prefer to use this opportunity to ingratiate myself with the military commander." Godunov was keenly interested in Pajari's report. The whole 'Junker' plant had been the object of extreme scrutiny since the Russians discovered the advanced research facility in the factory and it resulted in the decision to relocate a major portion of the plant. Presently, it was in the initial stages of being shipped to Russia. The train in question was only a small part of the factory.

The Kommissar was sorely tempted to secure the train for himself but he had enough on his plate the way it was. His trip to Switzerland had been successful and the single rail wagon with the penicillin was still on its way to Turkey.

Godunov reached for the field telephone on his desk and asked to be connected with Marshal Zhukov. Within a few minutes he had arranged a meeting with the Marshal who was greatly impressed by the quality of the information. The transport had been reported as missing and was already on his top priority list. To his surprise and satisfaction he heard that the new political member of his investigative team was already on top of it.

Marshal Zhukov was by nature a careful man and didn't trust too many of the political officers but Godunov's loyalty to Moscow was very well known and beyond any question. The meeting with the Russian Marshal proved to be very successful for Godunov. Zhukov assigned a team of sixty soldiers under the command of a captain to assist the Kommissar in securing the valuable freight.

"Where do we get a locomotive?" Pajari asked in bewilderment when Godunov ordered him to immediately get the transport rolling. There was no easy answer because most of the available engines were involved in taking POW transports to the east.

Nobody knew where the original locomotive was and Godunov implored Zhukov to give him an additional military convoy to enforce a requisition for an engine from any place he could find one.

The Marshal was only too happy to comply. He had the manpower available and the Kommissar had the political clout. Together, they should be able to get the train to its destination which was a rather small, but so far unknown town called Podberez'ye. It was located next to the Volga River, about 70 miles north of Moscow.

*****

Harold had been studying all morning when the door opened and Major Tesslov entered.

"Stop whatever you are doing and follow me." He glanced around the room and when he saw the open dictionary he took a crushed sheet of paper from his pocket and placed it between the pages before he closed it shut.

"Where are we going?" Harold was happy for the interruption and hoped to be involved in another exploit with the Major.

"You will be surprised. Go and get Alex. We need to hurry before one of our friends changes his mind."

There was no need to call Alex who was already waiting on the stairway.

Tesslov was driving the jeep and stepped on it as soon as they reached the open road to Spandau.

"The Kommissar succeeded in getting your father released." Tesslov came directly to the point of their trip. Harold was too surprised to say anything. He just stared in disbelief at Tesslov who continued. "Released into our custody, that is. Not released as a prisoner of war." He pointed at his breast pocket. "I have the transfer orders right here and I thought that you might want to come along. You can chat with your father on the way to the holding facility."

"What holding facility? How long does he have to stay there? You are not planning on sending him to Russia, I hope." Harold had found his tongue again. He was self-conscious when he realized that in his excitement he spoke German.

"Yeah, this is the part that puzzles me too. We don't have such an exclusive facility. We only have waiting sites for prisoners destined to go east."

They approached an American checkpoint and after the Major showed their identification they were allowed to proceed.

"These orders are confusing anyway. I just hope that your father does not escape before we are back in Russian territory."

If anyone was confused it was Harold. They could have stayed in Russian territory all the way to Spandau. There was no need to use the American access road to the political prison except that it presented a short cut.

Tesslov was in his natural element when he drove up to the entrance. He presented the transfer order and pointed proudly at Alex. "Take this fellow along and handcuff the prisoner to him. I don't wish to lose him."

The British captain in charge that day listened carefully to the Major. He seemed to be slightly annoyed that a Tatar was supposed to be a better guard than his own men.

"Keep this bear in the car. I don't want him in my facility. My men will bring the prisoner to the gate. Then he becomes your responsibility and you can chain him to whomever you wish."

He didn't even look at Harold who had a hard time sitting still.

The paperwork seemed to be in perfect order because the transfer happened without delay. Tesslov directed the prisoner to sit next to Alex on the back seat and Harold kept his head down until they were out of sight from the prison.

Herr Kellner didn't know what to expect. He had walked deeply bent over, afraid to look around. He was convinced that he was being transported to an interrogation pen. During the last week he had been sharing his cell with three other prisoners and all of them were scared beyond belief. There had been a rumor going around that they would be put to death by hanging. That is, if they were convicted of a major war crime. The mildest sentence was supposed to be ten years in solitary confinement.

The rumors changed from time to time but they never got any better.

"Pappa, look up, it's me, Harold."

It seemed that Herr Kellner was in a trance. His chin was still resting on his chest and his eyes were shut.

Harold turned in his seat and shook his father by the shoulders. "Open your eyes, Pappa, please."

Harold was afraid that his father was sick or had been drugged. But this was not the case. Herr Kellner was just plain tired. Tired of life and disillusioned with the outcome of the war. He had seen the inevitable coming, hoping all the time that he was wrong, until it was too late to run away. Besides, there was no place for him to run.

"Pappa." He heard the voice from his son again and slowly allowed himself to look around. If this was a dream it was awful real. He had a hard time adjusting his eyes when he recognized his son. He didn't know what to say and neither did Harold. They only looked into each other eyes, trying to give each other silent comfort without knowing how much time they had together.

"Harold, look up and show me the way to your friend's apartment." Tesslov was lost and needed directions.

"What friends? You mean the Beckers?" Harold hoped that he had heard the Major correctly.

"Yeah, I think that's their name. Since we don't have anything like a holding facility I figured we might as well make the most of the orders."

Harold watched dumbfounded as the Major ripped his father's transfer order to pieces and moments later the bits were lost among the dirt on the street.

"Darn it. Now I am without any identification for my prisoner, err... passenger, I meant to say." Tesslov turned his head to look at Harold's father. "Please, help me and disappear as fast as you can because I would not know how to explain your existence." He stopped the Jeep in front of Becker's apartment.

"Make it short, Harold. I need to maintain a certain time-frame and you can come back tonight."

Herr Kellner was finally coming out of his stupor and made motions to hug the Major who backed off and pointed at Harold. "Thank him. I am only a fumbling jailer who lost an inmate. In another minute I might have to look for him. So make it snappy."

"This is my father. I'll be back tonight." Frau Becker heard Harold's words as she opened the door. She didn't need any further explanation.

After a last hug, Harold was back in his seat.

"I will not forget what you did." He said to the Major who found his way back to the checkpoint.

"Let's not keep score. The ugly ones always know who they are." Tesslov had heard this phrase from Godunov and it was the first time that he had an opportunity to use it.

*****

It was still before noon when they returned to the Kommissar's office.

"Oh, you might wish to check your dictionary." He called behind Harold who went to his room to resume his studies.

The typewritten paper which Tesslov had left as a bookmark looked like it had been carried in someone's pocket for a long time. It was severely crumbled and Harold had to straighten it out on order to read it. It was a summation of pertinent facts about four Soviet soldiers. It listed all four of them by name and as sergeants as well as their unit and present location. However, one of the sergeants was released from active duty. The notes read *discharged due to accidental blindness.*

Harold tried to burn the physical descriptions as well as the names into his memory but then decided that it was easier to remember them as Wasserkopp number 1, with part of the left ear missing. Wasserkopp number 2, with a scar on his hand and Wasserkopp number 3 with a speech impediment.

He was certain that if he ever met them he would also

remember their names. At the present time he wanted to keep track of their regiment and unit and made himself some innocent notations among his language records.

"What a day." He proclaimed when he saw the Becker couple in the early evening. His latest ID allowed him to pass through the checkpoints without any questions from either side. The same held true for Alex who, like always, insisted on coming along.

"I'd like to suggest that you don't wake your father. We think he needs some rest or counseling or something. He seems to be void of any emotion and his short term memory is almost nonexistent. He asked us a few times about you but no matter what we told him, he kept on repeating his questions." Frau Becker informed him cautiously.

"How bad do you think he is? I mean, will he get back to normal? Where is he?" Harold had looked forward to the evening with his father and was now seriously concerned.

"Your father is resting upstairs in our neighbor's empty apartment," answered Herr Becker. "I saw symptoms like that before, mostly in WW I veterans. I think they even had a name for it."

"The name does not matter," interjected Frau Becker. "Your father needs rest first of all and I think that the knowledge that he is safe will also help him."

"What do you suggest I do?" Harold was almost afraid to ask. He didn't know of any relatives who could help. "He is all alone. Should I take him to a hospital?" He had noted on the way from the prison that his father was not the same man he knew.

"No. The hospitals are filled beyond capacity and he is not a medical emergency. I don't think that a hospital stay would help him anyway. He needs some quiet time without fear."

Frau Becker could see the anxiety in Harold's face.

"Don't worry, Harold, you and Karl helped us a lot and it is time that we are able to do something for you. Our neighbor's place is empty and they might never return. In any event, we are happy to take care of your father."

Harold let out a sigh of relief. "Thank you so much. I really don't know what to do."

Herr Becker noted that Harold was still concerned.

"Look, Harold, you did the impossible for your father. You

got him safely out of Spandau, so don't take his present condition as being anything more serious than it is. Your father might merely be in shock by the sudden reversal of his situation. He might be back to feeling normal in no time at all." He tried to alleviate Harold's distress.

"I hope that you are right, Herr Becker. Thanks for giving me hope."

He was ready to leave when Frau Becker surprised him with a note from Karl. "Sorry, I nearly forgot."

Harold opened the small envelope and looked at Alex who was sitting, as usual, on the floor by the door. "A letter from KaKa," he informed him. Alex got up and fingered the envelope. He could not read and waited for Harold to tell him more.

"KaKa is coming next week." This was all there was to the note, but Alex wanted to hear it again and again.

*****

An hour later they were back in their quarters. Captain Pajari had left a message for Harold to meet him in his office.

"We received information that there are several locomotives in a repair shed close to the Anhalter railroad station. The Kommissar went with Major Tesslov to ascertain whether or not they are useable. I have been ordered to conduct a fast inspection of our food convoys and you are to accompany me."

"What can I do to help?" asked Harold, not sure what a food inspection would entail.

"Nothing, but you are to stay close to me during the next week. Premier Stalin is coming within a few days and we are presently on high alert."

"Because of the Potsdam conference?"

"Maybe. I have no details other than that the food and fuel convoys have been ordered to leave Poland and are on the way west, to the Elbe River."

Pajari gathered his personal belongings and led the way to their car. It looked to Harold as if the Captain didn't plan to return. He could also see that the whole Russian sector of Berlin was primed for some kind of action. While he had been with Tesslov in Spandau and in West Berlin, the Soviets had moved additional infantry and tank units into the city.

The Captain elected to take the main thoroughfare in the

direction of Warsaw and then turned north. As they crossed the familiar road to Stettin, Harold saw to his amazement that all the traffic was being rerouted to secondary roads; all of them leading west.

"Start writing." Pajari handed Harold a notebook and called out the designations of the units they passed. Harold now knew why he had been ordered to assist the Captain; because he was also tasked with entering the various locations on an old German map.

"Are you still trying to tell me that you don't plan to move your troops all the way through Germany and France?" he inquired when he saw another fuel truck procession rolling towards the Elbe River.

Pajari turned his head as if surprised by Harold's remark. "What are you talking about? This is to demonstrate our strength and the readiness of our troops to Marshal Stalin."

"Right," answered Harold a little sarcastically. "How could I forget that Marshal Stalin does not know the strength of his own troops?"

When the Captain didn't answer he added, "I just remembered that Prime Minister Churchill and President Truman are also coming to Potsdam. Maybe you wish to give them a demonstration as well?"

Harold could almost feel that his question didn't sit right with the Captain. Before he had a chance to back pedal, Pajari answered with a twinkle in his eyes.

"Well, I don't know about that. Never-the-less, I share your anxiety. It does not look as peaceful as we are being led to believe."

Twenty

Godunov and Tesslov had been successful with their visit to the Anhalter station repair facility. Two of the locomotives were in a fairly good running shape but guarded by a group of soldiers and a sergeant from the second Ukrainian regiment. The commanding officer of the regiment was a colonel with the name of Igoshin. It was the same officer that Godunov suspected of organizing the sham operation of the medical and food depot along the Oder River.

However, the fake operation had not provided any evidence linking it directly to a specific regiment. Only the total absence of any clues together with the overly neat arrangements in the depot pointed to some fastidious mastermind.

"Take me to Colonel Igoshin," demanded Godunov approaching the sergeant.

"Colonel Igoshin is with the regiment in Potsdam and I cannot abandon my post."

"How long have you been here?" Godunov asked in a conversational tone.

"We arrived about ten hours ago."

"What are your exact orders?"

"To guard the operational locomotives until further orders are issued."

"Where have you been stationed during the past ten days?"

"With my regiment."

Godunov liked that the sergeant didn't volunteer any detailed information. He had no beef with a soldier doing his duty; however, he could not allow the sergeant to report back to the colonel.

"I have to retain you for further questioning. Right now you are suspected of theft and of plundering German assets." The Kommissar signaled the military unit from Marshal Zhukov to take the sergeant and his soldiers into custody.

"Wait", exclaimed the sergeant. His face had turned white and he felt weak in his stomach. To be arrested by a political officer was beyond his imagination. "I am not a thief. Please hear me out. I might have some useful information." He could hardly talk fast enough to be heard before he was led away.

Godunov smiled to himself. It was always the same. As soon as a soldier, or even an officer, was arrested by the NKVD and faced with the prospect of lifelong hard labor in Siberia, his memory improved. A few days of solitary confinement performed wonders.

"You will get your chance." The Kommissar turned away without looking back. He was satisfied with the arrest. It had bothered him that there was someone in the officer corps who seemed to be ahead of him. First the penicillin, then the replacement parts of machinery and now a train with airplane components. It was not only an insult to his intelligence but it was also his duty to stop this individual. To top it off, it was also severely hampering his own ambitions.

Sure, the trip to Switzerland with gold coins and precious stones had been successful but it was not nearly enough to secure his goals. Besides, some of the loot didn't even belong to him except that he would get a substantial reward (he called it a commission) for transporting it to a secure place.

A few hours later the engines arrived in Dessau. The Kommissar placed Major Tesslov in command to take the train to Podberez'ye and reported the successful mission to Marshal Zhukov.

"Excellent work," beamed the Russian marshal. "Premier Stalin will arrive tomorrow for the conference in Potsdam and I will personally report to him about your outstanding service and recommend you for a recognition."

Marshal Zhukov was more than pleased that his little problem had been solved.

Two days later Godunov established temporary quarters in

Potsdam. The party officials in Moscow had requested that he stay close to Premier Stalin during the conference. Officially he was supposed to provide additional security for the military commanders, but unofficially he was to report about the western mood during the negotiations.

"Here are your initial test papers." Pajari handed a whole bunch of paperwork to Harold.

"What kind of test?" They had just barely arrived in their new surroundings and Harold was hoping to get some time off to visit with his father and to see his friend during the next week.

"The Kommissar plans on sending you to a military cadet school," Pajari explained. "Don't worry too much about the general questions about your background. It is only a formality." He helped Harold to move a desk in front of a window. The new quarters were extensive and provided separate rooms for sleeping and studying. Even Alex had a room for himself but slept in front of Harold's door.

"What ever happened to Kete?" Harold asked Pajari. He had not seen Alex's buddy for some time.

"Kete is on an assignment in Simferopol. He is taking care of a personal matter for the Kommissar and I expect that he will join us again."

Harold wanted to ask another question regarding Simferopol but left well enough alone for the time being. However, he wondered what had happened to Godunov's shipment and he had to smile when he thought back to the time when he and his friend had arranged the valuable transport.

"Is there any chance I can see the Kommissar?" He still hadn't thanked Godunov for the release of his father.

"He will be very busy during the conference, but I will let him know that you wish to see him."

During the following days Harold was unable to leave Potsdam. The conference was in full swing and every day was filled with news and rumors. On the third evening, Godunov reported that Stalin was not in a good mood. The Premier was convinced that the western chiefs had delayed their move through France and the conquest of Germany on purpose. This had cost the Soviets millions of casualties while the western powers had taken their sweet time.

PARTNERS TO A DEGREE

"I wonder how this will end. President Truman is trying to steer us toward declaring war on Japan and this will cost us additional fatalities."

Godunov was also in a bad mood. He had been told that if the Soviets entered the war against Japan, he would be transferred to Manchuria. A vast, vast difference from Germany and an assignment he was not looking forward to.

A day later he had more news. "We agreed on a border adjustment. Russia will receive the eastern part of Poland and in return, Poland will receive a major portion of Germany. In fact, all of the German territory east of the Oder River will now belong to Poland."

Some of Godunov's reports were not so interesting to Harold. They centered on the various war reparation payments Germany was to provide to the Allies. It shocked him to hear that the Soviets demanded that Germany dismantle their second railroad spurs. They would be sent to Siberia to advance their rail system. Germany had a fully developed two spur system so that the trains could pass each other. By contrast, Russia had entire territories without any rail connections at all.

"Truman mentioned today, but only in passing, that the Americans had a new kind of bomb. Our intelligence service knows about it and it seems that the weapon is still in the experimental stage. Stalin thinks that if it was operational, the Americans would use it against Japan. Instead, the Western Allies pressured us again to join their war." Godunov reported a day later. He seemed disturbed by way the conference had progressed.

"Do you think that the conference will break apart?" Pajari asked a few days later when the Kommissar seemed to be fully disheartened. It was by now the end of July and the conference had begun on the 17th.

"No, not really. But the lack of a common enemy in Europe makes the negotiations very tough. Personally, I fear that Stalin has been pushed to the limits of his patience. The time will come when we will hardly talk to each other anymore."

Four days later, on the second day in August, the conference came to an end and the Kommissar announced the next morning that the Soviets would declare war against Japan. "I am not sure about the date, but I am ordered to be on the Manchurian border within a few days."

He turned to Harold. "Pajari will drive you tomorrow to visit your father and to see your friends. You may stay for a day or two and I will send the Captain to pick you up before I have to leave."

Harold had thanked the Kommissar a few days before and extended his hand to thank him once more.

"No need to go on, Harold. Your father's release was more due to his apparent innocence than to my efforts," he lied to Harold. In truth, he had nearly overextended himself in his struggle to secure freedom for Herr Kellner. In his opinion, Harold's father had simply been very good at his job but innocent of real war crimes. He couldn't help but think that if Herr Kellner was truly a war criminal, what would that make him? He was not too comfortable with the answer.

He had grown fond of Harold and he was certain that there was no future for a young man in Germany. Godunov wanted to give the boy some peace of mind before he took him to Russia.

*****

Harold jumped out of bed the next morning. "Alex, come on, we might see KaKa today." He yearned to find out how his father was doing and he also hoped that Karl would be there. He was not disappointed.

Pajari had been driving and before Harold could knock on the door it opened and Karl stood in the entrance. Both boys grinned at each other as they shook hands and exchanged their greetings. The Germans are not much for hugging but Alex didn't share their inhibitions. He lifted Karl off the ground and embraced him with tears in his eyes and it took a while before he let go of him. Karl's eyes were also moist from happiness.

"Welcome home," said Frau Becker as she led Harold to see his father. Herr Kellner laughed and cried as he recognized his son. He was in a much better shape and state of mind than a few days ago.

He wouldn't let go of Harold's hands and asked over and over again if Harold would stay with him. It was a very emotional reunion and much more heartfelt than a few days ago. Harold was amazed at his father's recovery and felt bad that he would have to leave him again, but, for a day they shared their feelings and memories.

"How have you been doing and why are you in Berlin?" Harold asked Karl after he had reported about the events of the past weeks.

"I am searching for a Lehrstelle, (apprenticeship) but I was unable to secure one in Westphalia. I didn't have much hope that my chances would be any better in Berlin, but it gave me the excuse to visit with the Becker's and to possibly see you."

"How did you manage to pass through the Russian zone?" asked Herr Kellner.

"Not much to it," laughed Karl. "I bribed the guards and once you are in Russian territory, it is relatively easy to enter West Berlin. But, I heard that the Soviets are about to tighten up so I might not be able to do this again."

"How is the food supply in western Germany?" Herr Becker wanted to know.

"Well, it is rationed, but we don't go hungry," Karl answered.

They talked way into the night and awakened to the news, the next morning, that the Americans had detonated an atom bomb over Hiroshima.

"Stay with us," implored Karl when Pajari showed up at noon on the next day to fetch Harold. "Come with me to West Germany. In due time we will find an apprenticeship together."

"No," answered Harold. He took Karl to the side so that his father couldn't hear him. "I have a chance to make it big and I intend to pursue it. Besides, I don't want to be taught by someone who might have been a Nazi. Did you hear about the horrors of the concentration camps?"

"Yes, of course," answered Karl. "But the papers make it out as if the Nazis only murdered the Jews and other minorities. We both know that they also murdered their own countrymen."

Harold shook his head. "Karl, we are not discussing who they murdered. We are talking about how we might be taught and that we may be brainwashed again by former Nazis and I want no part of it. Once is enough, thank you."

Karl looked at his friend. He knew that their ways would part forever and he feared that they might never see each other again.

"How do we stay in touch?" he asked.

"Give me your parents' and address I will find a way to

contact you. And, once I have an address of my own, you will be the first to know it." Harold had to fight to keep his emotions in check.

"Alright," said Karl. "If all else fails we can still keep in contact through the Beckers. And, if it means anything Harold, I worry about you, all alone in Russia."

Harold had to swallow hard. "It means more to me than you can imagine. But don't forget, you gave me a friend. Alex has not left my side since we parted and I fear that you will be more alone than I might ever be."

Karl looked sadly at his friend. "Time will tell, Harold, but if you ever need me...I'll be there."

Harold hated parting, especially from his father. His only consolation was the fact that his father was on the way to getting back to normal. He tried to make it as short as possible and for a moment he found fault with Alex who took the longest time letting go of Karl's hands.

"Step on it" he whispered under his breath to Pajari and then turned to his friends and his father. "I'll be back," he shouted as the Captain accelerated.

*****

Godunov was all packed up and almost ready to leave by the time they reached Potsdam. It was the 8th of August and the Soviet Union had declared war on Japan. The Kommissar had successfully used his influence to delay his departure to Manchuria. On the next day, August 9th, the Americans detonated another atom bomb over Nagasaki.

The papers claimed that the second bomb was used to prevent further bloodshed; that it was used to force Japan's hand. Somehow, Harold did not believe this to be true.

He had seen the combat readiness of the Soviet troops in Eastern Germany and Godunov had told him that they had not flinched when the first atom bomb detonated. However, when the Nagasaki bomb dropped, the Russian tanks turned around and the Soviet troops headed east. Harold saw it with his own eyes.

Truman had played a strong hand and Stalin blinked.

This was the reason, Godunov explained, that he was given a few days to visit with his daughter on the Crimean Peninsula. He took Harold along to enroll him into a Russian military cadet school.

Epilogue

Karl spent three years learning the pastry trade and after five years as a journeyman, he achieved his master designation.

In 1954, his father's sister who resided in New York, gave him the affidavit of support he needed to enter the United States as a legal immigrant. After the mandatory five-year waiting period he became a citizen of the United States. It was a decision he never regretted.

Karl chose to live a relatively quiet life and enjoyed traveling around the world.

Harold became an officer in the Russian Air Force and eventually avenged his mother. His life was the complete opposite of Karl's - one filled with danger and intrigue.

Over the years, Karl and Harold remained friends and often met in different international locations. On some occasions Karl would get to see his old friend Alex again.

When they met, Harold told Karl everything about his life and in between their visits, they would write to one another. Karl saved every note and letter Harold had ever sent to him. In Karl's mind, Harold led a much more interesting life and one that he thought he might like to write about some day. The two often joked that if one outlived the other, then the survivor would write a book and tell their stories.

Harold passed away at the age of 76 in the vicinity of Moscow. His passing was very difficult for Karl as the two had endured so much together - as young boys growing up in Germany and then fighting to survive the final days of World War II. His lifelong friend was gone but Karl did the one thing he loved doing most as a young boy - he took out his pen and he began to write.

Author's Note

This book took longer than expected to finish and to my readers, I apologize for the delay. Many of you were anxious to find out what happened next with Karl and contacted me to inquire about the release of Partners To A Degree, and for that I thank you. Your interest in the story helped me to keep writing even though life was presenting me with some unique personal challenges.

Writing Partners was a transition for me. On one hand I needed to bring Karl's story to an end as his life eventually became simple and uneventful in the years after the war ended. On the other hand, I wanted to bring Harold to the forefront of the story because his life changed dramatically and he will be the focus of my future books.

Aside from pursuing his own private agenda, Harold embraced the opportunities as well as the challenges that came his way as a protégé of an influential Russian Kommissar. He led a remarkable life and his greatest asset may have been his affinity for languages. He never stopped learning.

Over the years he obtained considerable insight into the Soviet political system, which he audaciously used to further his own career. While he died with the rank of a Russian officer, he was also an astute international trader.

Future books about Harold will be individual novels and the common thread will be historical events in which he, in one way or another, participated. Hopefully my stories will do him justice. They are based upon the notes and letters he sent to me and also the stories he told me when we met in different parts of the world.

As always, I enjoy keeping in touch with my readers and if you have any questions or comments about my books, please feel free to post them on my blog at www.horstchristian.com You are always welcome and I look forward to hearing from you.

If you enjoyed reading Partners To A Degree, please consider leaving a review. Your opinion is valuable not only to me, but to other readers as well.

Printed in Great Britain
by Amazon.co.uk, Ltd.,
Marston Gate.